Tales from Sleeping Moose
Vol. 1

A*LASKA-*

Mid-Century Pioneers

Nearly true stories told by Atwood Cutting

COPYRIGHT

Echo Hill Arts

For dear
Lorene and Elvin

My sincere thanks to David,
Audrey, April, MMAT, Marjorie,
Mr. Leon, Carolyn, Jacqueline,
Robert, Brandon, Kaye, and Sasha

I was born in Sleeping Moose, Alaska.
My mama was Kate Peters.
She used to tell me lots of stories about
living out in the bush.
She said they were all pretty much true.

Atwood Cutting

PAGE   CONTENTS

PROLOGUE:

Mama used to say, "Where the mud led off, and the road led on, that's where your daddy and I decided to settle."

To hear her tell it, that lack of a nice paved road was the root of all kinds of ills. "It brought out the worst in people, being so far away from civilization. But it also brought out the best," she was quick to add. "And those Goodmans were the best of the best."

Neil and Elsie Goodman were two real pioneers of the last century. They had homesteaded, and lived up on Round Top Mountain for a lot of years; which was a lucky thing because my parents knew *nothing* about surviving in the bush. They were Cheechakos, newcomers to Alaska, when they showed up on the Goodmans' doorstep that sunny July day in 1976. They had no idea what was in store.

Mama and papa met on the Alaska Marine Highway, on a ferry boat called the Tustumena. Each of them had been heading north to sample life on the Last Frontier. Finding that they shared an element of Romanticism and a set of old fashioned ideals, they decided to partner up and experience the adventure together. Not long after that, they eloped.

Newly married, the pair discovered Round Top Road quite by chance. While touring the Kenai Peninsula on their extended honeymoon, they came to an intriguing-looking hamlet consisting of half a dozen houses and a little gas station, all clustered around a log building with a flag pole out front. A sign nailed over the door read *Sleeping Moose Post Office*. It was the first settlement they had seen since they'd passed through Windsor Landing several miles back, where the Sterling highway first met up with the Kenai River. The couple had been mesmerized by glimpses of beautiful turquoise water running its course down those mountains. They'd seen lots of fishermen in waders, standing along the riverbank, but they hadn't seen many houses until now. On a whim, Tim turned the brand new Toyota™ Landcruiser onto an unmarked dirt trail that headed away from the post office and led up the hill because there was a hand painted sign advertising land for sale. It was a nice day. A detour couldn't hurt. Maybe there was some property up there that they might want to buy.

Their decision to explore that unremarkable-looking road would be revisited by Mama many times in the years to come; but right then, they were just following an impulse. They took that turnoff as a simple sunny day diversion. Luckily, they were young back then, with lots of energy, because it turned out to be a detour that would alter their lives right up into their idle years.

It'll take several books to tell you about all of the adventures my parents encountered at the end of that road; the weather, the mud, and the neighbors. I'll start with a sourdough couple named Goodman. If it hadn't been for those two, my parents might have frozen to death that very first autumn.

A.C.

CHAPTER 1
WHERE THE MUD LED OFF

The little dirt road wandered away through the woods. To what? Why not go up and see? It would be a minor detour on their way down to Homer, that day's intended destination. Why not indulge in an impromptu exploration? After all, it was a long July day, and the road looked dry enough.

Near the highway the road sent up little rooster tails of dust, and they drove with gusto for the first half mile. Tim Peters slowed down as soon as he started having to navigate a series of sizable mud holes. His bride, Kate, began holding onto the dashboard and twisting with every swerve of the car. Clearly the earth beneath these crowded spruce trees was still wet.

After about a mile of puddle maneuvering the amateur explorers came to another fork in the road, and took the one that had a second sign pointing down to a wooden bridge over a small creek. The old trestle's beams were rotten. Tim looked over at Kate and asked, "Shall we find out what's on the other side?"

His partner had her doubts. "Do you think it's safe to drive across? I can see holes right through in lots of places."

"Let's find out," he said. He hopped down out of their shiny green four wheel drive and turned the hubs on both front wheels. Then he got back in, shifted the car into 4WD and slowly edged it out onto two planks spanning the gap. Kate was looking out her window, down over the side of the car, studying the boards they were crossing. She stared straight down through the large gap between the planks and saw lazy swirls and eddies curling away downstream. Their precarious position caused her to pull up on the edge of her window, as if this would help to keep them from falling into the creek below. They made it across.

When they were safely on the far side, Tim gave the engine more gas and steered the little car up around a particularly slippery corner. Then he lost speed again when they cruised into more mud and more trees on the other side. The mud got deeper as the road took them through a flat and particularly soggy section at least a hundred yards long. They passed something made out of wood lodged in a ditch running along the edge of the road. Most of it lay buried, but enough of the old 2x8 boards poked out of the crusting mud to make a person curious. "Okay," said Kate. "I give up. What is that?"

"It looks like some kind of a homemade road grader for dragging this road smooth."

"Well it isn't working," Katie observed. Just then they bottomed out in the next deceptively deep mud hole. "Still, it's pretty cool to think that whoever lives up here fends for himself. It'd be nice to have this kind of privacy."

"Yes it would," Tim agreed. "But it would take a lot of work to live out here."

"It might be worth it," Kate said. "It's really beautiful."

The road wound through a lot more spruce trees and muddy patches before starting to climb a steep straight grade. Tim steered up the hill. The dirt road now ran between a wire fence bounding the south edge of a pasture, and several big rocks sticking out of the now-dry section of road. The possibility of a good view on top was looking promising, and the two leaned forward.

When they popped up onto a big flat space and Tim took his foot off the accelerator, what they saw looked like a haphazard farmyard. A big silver cargo truck served as a fence across one side of the yard, and a long red cattle trailer closed the gap between the barn and the pasture. There was a privy out near a newer-looking shed that could have been a hen house. A few chickens scratched at the dirt in front of it. Behind the privy was a paddock where a small flock of sheep stopped grazing, and stood looking at the new arrivals. Ancient tractors and pieces of rusting equipment lay here and there between the oversized barn and a little house shaped like a Hostess® Twinkie. A stovepipe stuck out of one sloping side wall of the house, sending puffs of smoke upward into a blue sky.

The view beyond was fantastic: miles of untamed Alaskan wilderness.

As their car coasted to a stop, an old man opened the glass-paned door and stepped outside. He looked his visitors over, and then smiled. Katie and Tim did the same. The fellow had to be at least sixty years old. Dressed in Levi's® and boots and a plaid shirt with abalone-snap breast pockets, he appeared to be the genuine article. He was bowlegged, like maybe he'd done a lot of horse riding; and his silver head fit perfectly into a big white cowboy hat. When he got close, Kate could see that his eyes were an honest-looking blue. The way they shone when he smiled made her want to like this man from the get-go.

"Howdy," he said, touching the brim of his Stetson®. "Can I help you folks?" He really sounded like a cowboy, talking slow and relaxed like he had all day. And maybe he did.

Kate turned around full circle, taking in the dynamics of this remote setting of rolling hills and snow covered peaks and one round mountain looming straight ahead. It was pure Alaska. Tim stretched out his hand to shake. Then, when Tim stepped back, she shook hands with the man.

"The name's Goodman," the cowboy said.

"Peters," Tim responded.

Right away, the man invited the couple inside to meet his wife.

Their home was a simple World War II Quonset® hut, with one window in each end, and the one glass door, through which they had just entered. A kitchen counter with a matching shelf above took up most of one side. The whole front end of the room was taken up by another counter that housed a mid-century style tin sink unit. Both counters were skirted with gingham. A mid-century vintage Formica® table separated the kitchen area from the living room area. There were four bent steel chairs positioned around it. The whole place measured no more than 12x24 feet, and maybe less. A sagging double bed was against the far end, and extra sets of denims and shirts hung on a row of nails protruding from the back wall. Two easy chairs and a reading light set close to the furnace filled the middle of the room. That was everything there was to this mountain home. Since she didn't see a door leading off to a bathroom, Kate guessed these folks must still use that privy across the yard.

"This here's my other half, Elsie," the cowboy said. "We came up here and homesteaded back in '58."

Apparently, a homesteader's work was never done because the fellow told them he hadn't gotten around to building their real house yet...and they'd been living in this tiny shack for eighteen years.

The four talked for a few minutes before Tim inquired about purchasing land nearby. Goodman smiled. "I've got some land up there I might be able to sell you," he said.

"There's a good house site for you to build on, if you're of a mind to." He offered to take the couple further up the mountain. "The road stops at the top edge of our homestead. Nothing beyond there but wilderness," he told them.

Tim and Kate were intrigued by such a serendipitous opportunity. The view was so good from where they were right then; how much better would it be even higher up? So they accepted the cowboy's invite to see what they could see.

Elsie said, "You three go ahead. I'll stay here and wash up the dishes. I don't like to go-molly them."

At a questioning look from Kate she added, "That's a trick the Mormon folks use. They go-molly their dishes, hiding 'em 'til later so's they can get to their socials in a hurry. But I can't see doing that," she concluded, by way of explanation.

The trio went outside and climbed into Neil's old Jeep. The pickup bounced out of the yard, and continued across another three quarters of a mile of rough pasture until they arrived at the very top edge of the Goodman's hundred and sixty acre spread. When they got out of the farm truck, the panorama below rivaled Yosemite. Where the pasture track ended there was nothing but thousands of acres of uninhabited grazing lease land. A single, gnarly bear trail wound away into the trees.

"No one lives back there?" Tim asked.

"Indians might have once I suppose, but no one lives there now," Goodman said.

The whole thing looked like an adventure waiting to happen. And it had been waiting specifically for Tim and Kate. One look, and they decided right then and there to pool their money and buy the back forty of the homestead.

The couple held hands, stepped up to Neil and declared, "We'll take it!"

***

"Have you got a calculator?" Tim was asking as the three entered the Quonset hut through the antique glass door.

"No, but I've got a pencil and paper," the silver-haired cowboy said.

"Have a seat, why don't you? Say, Elsie can you cut us some o' that pie? We're celebrating! These nice folks here are buying the back forty!"

13

"Why sure," his wife said with a big smile. "...Oh, my! Well, welcome to Round Top Mountain!" Elsie crossed to the long plank counter and started carving four big pieces out of her freshly baked work of art. The two men sat down at the other end of the table, and started scratching out some mathematical equations, eventually agreeing upon a payment schedule.

"Please call me Kate," the young Mrs. Peters said, as she chose the smallest of the bent steel chairs and sat. She could smell sweetened rhubarb, an aroma she hadn't come across since she was a little girl. "I think I smell rhubarb," she said to Mrs. Goodman. "My mother used to bake rhubarb pies. Some people put strawberries in them, but she didn't."

"This is plain rhubarb," the cook said.

"That's my very favorite!" Kate exclaimed. Too excited to sit still, the young guest couldn't help but bounce in her springy steel chair. She looked around with pleasure at the utilitarian, yet inviting home they had discovered at the end of this isolated road. Everything felt good.

From that day forward, whenever they visited the Goodmans Kate always sat in that bouncy chair. She vowed as how those times made for some of the happiest memories of her life.

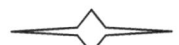

"Okay. Let's get your full names," Neil said as he started writing up a formal agreement on a clean sheet of paper.

"Timothy David Peters and Katherine Cutting Peters," Tim said solemnly.

Neil carefully lettered out all the information, and then folded up the paper and stuffed it into his abalone snap shirtfront pocket. "We can go on into town later to record the deed. But this rhubarb pie of Elsie's is a-callin' to us right now, don't you reckon?"

"Definitely!" Kate blurted.

While they ate pie, Neil answered their questions about homesteading and told them a bit about the area. He explained to them about how they'd had to 'prove up,' by putting five acres into cultivation. "To do that," he said, "we needed a barn. And to build a barn, we needed to build a saw mill first." And so on until, there they were, eighteen years older, with a lot of dusty furniture waiting for a living room to put it in. But for now, the couch sat in the barn, while Neil and Elsie Goodman lived in this cozy, if tight house. Neil said maybe one day they'd hook up hot water; but in 1976, cold running water was as far as they'd gotten.

Elsie looked pretty content. "I wouldn't mind having a second room someday," she admitted to

Kate, "so I could go to bed while Neil's visiting with the neighbors."

"Neighbors?"

"Oh, there's a few folks live up this way. There's a pair of brothers on the other side of the flat down over there," she pointed out through the glass door at a hill far away. Kate looked, but she couldn't see a house.

"We don't socialize with them much, though. And there's a couple that lives over on the next ridge over there." She pointed west. "They homesteaded, like us. We usually get together a couple of times a year; before they leave for the lumber camp, and whenever they get back. Neil likes to talk politics with 'em. And there's a nice couple down close to the highway. You drove past their place on your way in.

"We did see a little farm," Kate remembered. "A nice garden, and some goats."

"Yup, that's it. Young folks. You'll like 'em."

That first conversation over a warm piece of pie launched a friendship that Mama still talked about years later; long after the Goodmans had moved off and left the state. Before they departed though, the old-timers bailed the newcomers out of more than one soft spot, and laid down a foundation of backwoods wisdom that would help this next generation of pioneers stay above ground for a long time.

A.C.

Good times at the Twinkie

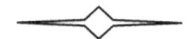

CHAPTER 2
HOUSEWARMING

They planned to build a cabin. They planned it on a napkin. It would be a small log cabin. Kate wanted to have a little window in the back wall so she could watch the squirrels playing outside in the alder grove. She thought she could make do with a campfire on the dirt floor just inside the door and an open hole in the ceiling for smoke to escape. After all, they were only going to be living in it until they had the big house built, which they figured would be about a year.

Earlier that day they'd found a pressed-down patch of grass in the exact shape of a moose. You could see the perfect outline of the body, with the head and neck stretched out full-length. "If this isn't a sign, I don't know what is," she'd said, since the town below was called Sleeping Moose. That smart moose had chosen the perfect spot: a nice windbreak to the north, and a panoramic view of the Chugach Range, Tustumena Lake, and the ice capped Kenai Fjords way off to the south. Kate thought they should build their real house right there.

Their new home town wasn't much of a town, really; just a dry goods store/post office and one little Tesoro™ gas station. "General Delivery" would be their address, and the Goodmans, three-quarters of a mile below, would be their closest neighbors. After that, their next human neighbors would live four miles away by dirt road. Maybe you could take a shortcut across the flat, but that wasn't easy unless you were a moose. Good and private! Kate was picturing herself dancing in the summer sunshine out in front of their little cabin. Tim was envisioning himself as Jack London, who built a house to winter in until he could sail down the Yukon to reach the Klondike and mine material for all of his books. That sounded fun, too. "Do you think we can really do that?" she'd queried, because she knew that any construction project she undertook would probably end up looking like--- and lasting about as long as---a treehouse.

"If anyone can do it, we can," Tim had answered. And that was how they started.

That night they slept under the stars.

Honeymoon Cottage at the end of the road

***

"It's time to go shopping. Let's head on down to Footprint. Hopefully there's a hardware store there," Tim suggested. Located twenty miles from Sleeping Moose, Footprint was the biggest town around. It wasn't huge, but Neil told them it had a lot more stores than Sleeping Moose. Footprint sat all alone out in the middle of about a thousand square miles of moose and lake-strewn marshland. Soldotna was another twenty miles further west. If they couldn't find what they needed in Footprint, then a supply run to Soldotna would probably take all day.

"Hopefully there's a bigger grocery store," Kate added. "The selection at the general store here in Sleeping Moose is pretty disappointing."

***

"Got time for some coffee?" Neil intercepted them as they drove through the farmyard on their way to town. The two had a thousand plans for the day, but it might be a nice thing to stop in for a minute. The couple probably didn't get a lot of company up that way.

"Sure," Tim said. "That'd be great." They got out of their rig and followed Neil inside.

"We can only stay for a few minutes. We've got a lot to do today," Kate said, gently cautioning that they wouldn't be there for long.

"Uh-huh," Neil said. He called in as he opened the door, "Look here, Elsie. We've got company!"

Elsie glanced up from tending the furnace as they entered.

"Have you got any of that pie left?" he asked her.

"No," she said, smiling right at Kate, "but I baked another rhubarb pie this morning, just in case you two were to come by." She finished rearranging the coal embers, shut the furnace door and washed her hands off with cold water. Then she started cutting up the still-warm pie.

Kate watched the aging cowgirl's back as she fixed up the plates, noting first the stiff back brace she wore, then the farm pants and shirt, and the pointed boots that held her leggings tight against her ankles. Kate studied the woman's raven black hair, cut short in back like a man's, but with two little twirls of hair wrapping forward around her ears. Then she homed in on Elsie's dangly turquoise earrings and--when she turned around--her bright red lipstick! "Welcome to Alaska," Kate silently mused, "Where men are men and women wear pants...and sometimes they wear lipstick!"

As Elsie slid into a chair beside her at the table and took her first bite of pie, Kate asked, "How did you folks get your supplies up here back in the old days?"

"We used to pack the groceries up on snowshoes, and drag everything else up behind the tractor," Elsie said. Her voice was a pleasant baritone, and matter of fact. No hint that their lifestyle had been the least bit difficult or out of the ordinary.

"I guess you were glad when they invented snowmobiles," Kate ventured.

"Oh my, yes!" Elsie assured her. "That made things a lot easier, I'll tell you."

"Where did you two come from, before you homesteaded here in Alaska?" Tim asked.

"Arizona," Neil volunteered. "Elsie's dad was a cattle rancher, and so was mine. When we hitched up, we started our own cattle operation outside of Payson...Did fine, too, 'til the government took it all away with some eminent domain malarkey."

Kate listened to the cowboy while her thoughts were fixed on Elsie. Not a gray streak anywhere on her head. She had to be nearly sixty. Her eyes were grayish blue. Her skin was fair. Could she be part Indian? The earrings looked Native-made. ...She wore lipstick and earrings. Why? Had she gotten dressed just up for them? It was possible. After nearly two decades, the woman might be excited to finally have neighbors close by. How had she avoided cabin fever and lonesomeness for all that time? How would Kate do in a similar situation? Would she be as strong as this pioneer's wife? Tim was strong; but Kate was more of an artist. Would she be determined enough to make it up there, the way Elsie had? Kate decided she'd do well to take a few lessons from this pair, and from Elsie especially, as she was the perfect role model.

After two pieces of pie and three cups of coffee each, the young couple inched their way out the door, and recommenced their journey into town. By the time they had returned home to the spot where the moose once slept and unloaded all their new gear, it was getting dark and starting to drizzle. They opted to bed down in the back of their water tight covered wagon instead of sleeping in the rain.

***

The next morning the newlyweds painfully unfolded their knees and crumpled bodies and slowly emerged from the Toyota's cramped backseat. The rain had stopped, and they were met by a glorious new day. "Today we start to build our house!" Tim announced with a huge smile.

Excited, Kate hummed as she made oatmeal on the shiny new Coleman® stove, purchased at the supply store in Footprint. They had also bought two spoons, two metal bowls, two tin cups, a speckled blue coffee pot, a small white ceramic cooking pan and a five-gallon container. And now they had five gallons of water in it, which they had gotten from the public spigot in front of the Sleeping Moose post office. What more could a bride ask?

Tim pulled off the tarp protecting their tools, and began doing something with the new chainsaw. He wiggled the chain back and forth, filing a tooth from time to time and giving the whole thing a tweak every so often. "Let's hope we don't get any more rain until we've finished the cabin," he said.

"That was terrible last night," Kate agreed. "Sleeping all crunched up in the car, I couldn't straighten my legs all night. It hurts my knees to squat by this stove."

"Maybe we can make a little table for you today," Tim suggested.

"That would be good. And the sooner we finish the cabin, the better," Kate added.

When breakfast was ready they gulped down oatmeal, had one cup of coffee each, rinsed out their bowls and their mouths--which were gritty with "cowboy" coffee grounds--and gathered up the tools they'd be using for their first day of lumberjacking.

"Let's do it!" Tim said.

"I'm ready!" Katie cheered.

Off they went, in search of a few flat rocks and a lot of straight trees.

By evening they had all four cornerstones set, plus two more to hold up the door frame. The cabin would rest on these boulders, which they had dropped down into the subsoil and wrestled fairly flat in the mud. Tomorrow they would start cutting trees for the log walls of their temporary home. "I'd also like to start work on an outhouse," Kate said.

"Huh?"

"We're going to need an outhouse," she repeated.

"Let's get ourselves a house, first. We can go in the alder grove for a while."

"Maybe, but I'd prefer it if we designated a spot as soon as possible. I don't want to step in anything in the dark."

That night a good rain fell. At Kate's suggestion, they postponed the logging expedition for the morning and spent half of the day digging a huge privy hole in the softened earth. After a couple of peanut butter and jelly sandwiches they went out to scout for, and cut down their first trees. Home at dusk with four trees chained behind their little green tank, they were jubilant. They had actually begun to build a house!

***

It rained solidly for the next ten days and nights. Tim and Kate went out anyway. They worked in the woods logging, bucking and dragging the day's harvest of limbed trees back to the cabin site, and then crawled into their four-foot square luggage area for another miserable, cramped night. One thing the Toyota was really good for was dragging home the cut and readied logs. One thing it was really bad for was sleeping in!

Luckily, Tim was turning out to be quite a handy fellow. He had worked construction and maintenance in his hometown before he left for Alaska, and he brought a lot of practical experience to the table. This was good, since Kate had no such skills. She had been a performing artist, a singer and a dancer up until the day she'd decided to quit show business and "go to see the elephant," as her mother had put it. Kate hoped she was holding up her end of the bargain. She might not know much about mechanical matters, but she was smart and she could lift heavy things. They made a good team.

As soon as they had hauled a few logs up to the site, Tim would use both chisel and chainsaw to notch the ends, and Kate would help him lift and set a round of logs on top of the layer from the day before. Their day's work done, they'd sit on a couple of stumps set out under the sky (or in the car if it was raining,) and dine on corned beef hash. Then Kate would rinse the single cooking pan and their two bowls, while Tim covered up the tools; and they would both climb into the back of their little car and try to sleep.

They went to bed exhausted each night, and woke up in pain each morning. Katie couldn't imagine how pioneers and sailors could sleep in those tiny beds back then. She couldn't wait for that wonderful day when they would finally move out of the car and into the cabin.

***

After five days the walls stood almost waist high. Tim cut a doorway into the south side, and they stood back to admire their progress. It looked good. The logs wouldn't need peeling since this would be their home for such a short time, but maybe some chinking would help to keep the wind out.

Limbing, Hauling,
Dreaming, Fantasizing,
Building, Improvising

The little creek down in the woods was loaded with mossy rocks. When the rain let up, Tim and Kate went moss collecting. Tim stood guard with the new shotgun tucked under his slicker, while "his woman" picked moss and stuffed it into a plastic bag. When the saturated mist gathered and dribbled off the end of her chin she used her flannel sleeve to wipe her nose, knowing that the bears wouldn't tell. "We could call this 'Cutting Creek' in honor of my family," she suggested. And so it was.

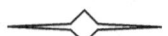

Katie wrote to her mother in Hawaii, updating her with highlights of their arctic adventure.

August 20, 1976–Dear Mamasan,

You'd love this place. I've been gathering moss and chinking the walls with it, like a pioneer woman in a sod house out on the plains. Tim gave me a hatchet lesson the other day. Slipped and nearly cut his off his leg in the process. (Not a deep cut, but we both got an idea of how careful we need to be way out here.) ...But this is all so much fun!

P.S. We're sleeping in our car until we get the cabin finished. Luckily we bought a Toyota with 4x4 knobs on the wheel hubs, and a heavy-duty winch on the front bumper. I call it the "impregnable rolling fortress" because it'll go anywhere and never

***

It took another three days to get the walls up to armpit height. This made a total of eight rainy nights sleeping and eating in the little covered wagon. They joked that they would be a pair of jack-in-the-boxes by the time they finally got to sleep stretched out straight again.

On the ninth day Tim had a brainstorm.

"Let's make the roof take off in a slant right from here, and call it done," he suggested.

"Won't it look funny?"

"Who cares? It just needs to be dry."

Kate said, "Fine," and they switched to vertical log poles and finished the place in just two more quick days. So what if it only looked like half a cabin? It could be slept in; and at that moment that's what really mattered. Besides, they'd be moving up into their real house shortly.

As soon as Tim had tacked a layer of green roofing paper on top, they constructed a hasty bed of plywood on cinder blocks. Two quilts later and, "Ta-da!" they'd be stretching out straight tonight!

Tim built one wide triangular shelf in the corner for the Coleman camp stove, and another shelf underneath for the bowls, and cups, and all of their food, which was mostly peanut butter, jelly, bread, canned corn beef, instant potatoes, onions, oatmeal, raisins, brown sugar, coffee, powdered lemonade, and powdered milk. By now they had added two more white enameled sauce pans and one well-used cast iron frying pan. Windsor Landing had lots of great garage sales. Katie decorated her new kitchen by hanging all four pans in descending sizes from descending nails in the descending log wall above. Next they ran a couple of clothes shelves along the back wall, just above the bed. Carpentry tools would get the whole end wall, and Neil's G.I. stove would take up the last corner. The bare metal fire box had been a surprise housewarming gift from Neil Goodman. He'd had it sitting out in back of his barn for a decade or two, probably waiting for the house. When he dug it out he said he thought the new homesteaders would need it sooner or later.

Kate resisted his gift for a half a second, because it wasn't the fire pit in the dirt floor that she'd been picturing. But Tim said, "Yes," and installed it in the corner between the bed and the front door. He cut a hole in the highest corner of the slanted roof and stuck a length of stovepipe up through it. And now they had a living room! Kate wedged two concrete blocks between the wood stove and the bed, and hoped that would prevent any spontaneous combustion. It was pretty close quarters in there.

The last home improvement Tim made was to pound a pair of spikes into the lintel over the door. He twisted a sock around each peg, and hung the shotgun from them. Katie had fainted the day she was holding up that lintel, waiting while Tim labored to get it attached to something.

"Tim, I feel--." Boom! She'd been on the ground before she knew it. And now, Tim was hanging their means of protection from it. They had really arrived!

There wasn't room for one more thing inside that cabin. If one of them wanted to go outside, the other one was obliged to step onto the bed so the opening door could clear.

"It's not as big as I thought it was gonna' be," Tim said, when they were finally standing all the way inside the fully-appointed cabin, and the door was shut.

"I guess we probably should have cut the logs a little longer, to allow for the notching."

It was dark in there, too. The plywood door with insulation stapled to the inside provided no light. In fact, the only place they could see light was through the spaces between the vertical wall logs.

"Maybe we can cut a window in the door," Katie suggested. "More light might help."

"Yeah, I'll do that tomorrow. But this'll do for tonight. At least we'll be sleeping out straight."

"That's right, big boy! We'll sleep like kings!"

Kate was chattering with excitement. "It's our very first home, and we built it ourselves. Don't you just love it? ...I do! What shall we name it? ...How about Half Dome? It kind of reminds me of Half Dome, the way it cuts off in front."

"I'd rather call it Honeymoon Cottage."

"A fine name," Kate agreed instantly. Which it really was.

Measuring the dimensions, they found that their little "Honeymoon Cottage" was just shy of eight feet by eight feet.

"It's a perfect starter home," Kate said, totally delighted.

They took turns half-dragging each other over the threshold before bedding down for their first good sleep in ages. Heaven!

***

The temperature dropped steadily as they slept, approaching the freezing point the way the heating kettle sneaks up on the unsuspecting frog. Long before dawn the rain switched from gray sleet to white snow, and heavy flakes set about feverishly erasing the road and covering all of the supplies still stored outside. When they woke in the morning and pulled open the big winter door, there was nothing to be seen; nothing at all. Just a blank Cinerama® screen, like the one Kate had seen *2001: A Space Odyssey* in back home. This scenery wrapped around like that now, completely engulfing them.

Only ten hours earlier, the friendly fireweeds had been their company. Now, in the blink of an eye, the entire landscape had turned barren and bitter. Their glorious view was mysteriously vacant.

The spectacular horizon had vaporized. There was nothing visible out there but a milky galaxy swirling in a lusty wind. Tim stood staring out at the nothing for so long that Kate finally had to begin slapping her arms together to keep warm. "Too bad we didn't get around to gathering up some firewood before now," she said with belated insight.

But her partner pushed the door closed and gave her a confident grin. "No problem," he said. "I saw lots of dead wood up in the windbreak. Let's go get some."

"Okay, sounds good. And let's have some oatmeal first. I want to try out my new kitchen."

Tim sat back down on the bed, leaned against the clothes shelf, and folded his hands behind his head. "Perfect. I can sharpen the saw while you cook the oatmeal."

"Deal." She took a pan off of its nail, opened the door (with Tim swiveling his legs out of the way) and stepped out to pour some water from the five gallon can that sat on a shelf outside the door. She had to break the can away from its mooring, and she heard several chunks of ice bang together inside. Tilting the can, she poured a trickle of water out between the ice chunks, just enough to fill the white saucepan and the blue coffeepot.

"Where will we store our water, to keep it from freeing? Under the bed?" she asked, once she was back inside.

"Let's just worry about getting some firewood, right now."

That made Kate start wondering where they would keep the firewood, as well.

Ten minutes later, with hands finally warmed beside the camp stove; they were sitting on the front edge of their bed, staring at the silver-foiled insulation stapled to the door, eating hot mush.

"I still think a window in this door might be a good idea," Kate suggested again. Before Tim could answer, she sat up straight and seemed to be listening hard. "...Do you hear something?"

Tim stopped eating, his spoon in mid-air, and together the pair listened with something like a faint fear, as the vague grinding noise grew stronger through the gusting winds.

"That's not a bear, is it?" she asked her husband, who had been born and raised in the city and knew no more about the man eaters than she.

"No," Tim said. "It sounds like something mechanical." He stood up to look outside.

Kate got up and stood behind her protector as he edged the big door open a crack and peeked out. There was nothing visible out there, but the growling roar was getting closer.

Kate squinted out over Tim's shoulder, and then she saw a plume of black smoke swirl out of the opaque world in front of them.

Still closer now, the clanking was louder…

Two tense seconds later a gargantuan yellow monster emerged from the white void.

"It's a bulldozer!" Tim cried, totally surprised, and visibly relieved.

The earthmover was chewing its way steadily toward them, etching out a new road where the surprise blizzard had taken away the first one.

"Neil!" Tim recognized the fellow almost immediately.

Neil waved down at the amazed pair, and brought his D-6 Caterpillar® to a halt. "Good morning!" he shouted against the wind. "I thought you two might be ready for the other half of your housewarming gift now." He gestured toward a silvery, dead spruce tree chained to the back of his puffing machine.

"Oh gosh Neil, you brought us firewood! How perfect! Thank you so much!"

"Come on in. We've got coffee!" They were both talking to him at once, and the roaring wind was carrying their words away toward oblivion but he seemed to get the idea.

"Sure. …For a minute."

The aging man climbed down off the dozer without much trouble, and left his diesel Cat idling. He and Tim broke snow over to the front of the chained tree. The chain had tightened during the trip up, so they had to wrestle with it for a while before they finally got the chokehold loose and the silvery skeleton rested in the snow. His delivery complete, Neil ducked under the low lintel and entered their tiny abode. Kate poured some cowboy coffee into a hastily rinsed cup and handed it to Neil. Then she sat down on the edge of the bed beside him. Tim grabbed the chainsaw, and went back outside to make firewood out of the dead timber. Then Kate, a Girl Scout at heart, grabbed up paper and wood splinters and started laying a fire on the round grate in the bottom of the empty G.I. stove. She wanted to have the kindling ready for some real wood by the time Tim came back inside.

***

"How can we thank you enough?" Kate gushed. The three were now standing in a tight circle, staring straight down into the open G.I. stove, watching the thin flames begin to catch onto the seasoned wood.

"Yeah, you really saved us today," Tim said. He slid the round slab of metal that served as a stove lid back on top of the barrel, and bent to adjust the little air door at the bottom.

"No need to thank me," Neil scoffed. "It's good to finally have some fresh young neighbors to move in. Most of the folks who come up here to the end of the road are sort o' rough, I guess you might say."

That comment hung over the cabin until Neil finally broke his own silence. "But you'll find out for yourself pretty soon, I reckon. There's a going away party over at the Curd place next Saturday. You can come along with us and meet everybody all at once. They're a bunch o' characters, that's for sure. You should get quite a kick out of 'em."

Neil stayed for a few more minutes, talking mostly about the weather, and the grizzlies.

"They come right through here every spring and fall." Then he invited the newlyweds to come down for dinner (which turned out to be lunch) at one o'clock. That was the big meal of the day for cowboys and farmers, alike. "Steak and biscuits," was how Neil described it.

"...Yup, just watch out for 'em," Goodman said, by way of wrapping up his yarns for that quick visit. "They're out there, alright. But they won't bother you, if you just stay out o' their way."

Then their generous neighbor stood, zipped up his Carhartt® coveralls, put on his wool hat and mittens, tipped his head a little, and exited the cabin. He climbed up onto his bulldozer, pulled the lever to swing it into gear, and headed home. For the second time, he plowed out their three-quarters of a mile of drifting driveway as he went. Kate pictured Elsie waiting for her husband, ready with a cup of hot Ovaltine as soon as he emerged from the tempest. Then she thought about what the sourdough had said. 'They won't bother you, if you just stay out o' their way.' Had he been talking about the bears, or the neighbors?

September 1, 1976 -- Dear Mamasan,

After sleeping cramped up in the car for almost two weeks, last night we slept in our new log cabin! Just in time too, because last night it snowed! We'll live here until we build the main house further up the hill. I figure we should be done with that sometime next year, but for now we're happy to be warm and dry. We still need to build a place to store our water and our firewood. And we need an outhouse. But things are getting more comfortable around here every day. The folks we bought our land from are so nice! Wait 'til you meet them. By the way, when can you come up to visit?

At one o'clock by Tim's watch they were driving the road Neil had just cleared for them down to the Goodmans.' The snow berm on either side was shoulder high and the roadbed itself was pretty choppy, but the four wheel drive was handling it well. So maybe getting home in winter wasn't going to be so tough, after all. As long as Neil kept the road plowed up to their house, they had nothing to worry about. But they might want to get a snowmobile at some later point. They'd have to see.

As soon as their rig had cleared the last spruce tree and entered the flat space in front of the Twinkie house, someone dressed like a cowboy appeared behind the glass door. Which one was it? They both dressed the same. When the door opened, it was Neil who beckoned them inside. They entered, took off their Carhartt coats and wool hats, and sat down at the table. Kate chose the bouncy chair, and started her comfortable rocking. The whole house smelled wonderful. There was something with cinnamon and sugar baking in the oven, and that made the two hungry in a hurry.

That first 'dinner' that Elsie cooked up for them was a masterpiece of pork chops, potatoes, home canned tomatoes, peas, corn, hot gravy, apple sauce, biscuits with butter and honey, and cinnamon turnovers for dessert.

When everyone was stuffed, Neil leaned back, rubbed his barrel chest, uncapped a Rolaids® bottle that seemed at home right there on the dining table, and offered them around. Nobody took one, so he popped a handful of the calcium pills into his mouth and chewed them up. Now he was ready for one last cup of tea and a little neighborly talk. It turned out he was of the John Birch Society persuasion, and he wanted folks to know all about the recently-exposed Rockefeller conspiracy. Elsie started heating water for dishes in a big aluminum kettle, and Kate offered to help. The two women stood side by side at the sink, washing and drying the dishes, looking out the window at the white winter scene, and listening to Neil's political argument. For Kate it was all new information, but she figured Elsie had probably heard it a few times before. No wonder she wanted a house with a second room!

The Peters left the Goodmans' quite a while later, all informed about the terrible truth that the world was being manipulated by the helpful-sounding, but insidiously-intentioned Tri-Lateral Commission. They got home just in time to stoke the cooling fire with an infusion of dry wood.

The reality of that first surprise snow had moved firewood right up to the top of their 'to do' list, even before an outhouse!

***

The next gift from Neil and Elsie was a load of coal, which they delivered two days later. They claimed that most of the locals gathered their coal right off the beach over in Kenai. "It's free for the taking," Neil assured them. "We'll show you where it floats ashore."

That sounded easy.

All this author can say about that story is she's lucky the Goodmans took their tradition of housewarming so seriously. If they hadn't, her parents might've been dead after that first night, and she wouldn't be here today, telling you this very nearly true story!

A.C.

Neil's G.I. stove sure did come in handy
that first winter up on the mountain.

The six mile "driveway"

CHAPTER 3
MEET THE NEIGHBORS

"Are you about ready?" Tim had his hand on the door latch.

"I'm ready," Kate said as she zipped her down vest. She slipped into her felt lined Sorrel® boots and grabbed her wool hat. It was raining, as it had been for most of the week. Kate crossed the muddy yard in a few giant steps, using the flattened slices of logs that she'd placed in a line, like stepping stones.

Although the snow had all but disappeared after that first surprise blizzard, Tim and Kate had spent a good part of each day since, cutting and hauling firewood back to the cabin. They would be prepared next time. They had it all stacked next to the wall outside, under a tarp. A woodshed was high on the list; but now it didn't seem as urgent as getting a privy with a seat. That would be their next project, for sure!

Bush living had a way of reducing one's requirements to a base level; with survival as the overriding concern, and transportation a strong second. Rural residents worried more about keeping alive, and less about keeping clean. Very few houses outside of town had running water, because the perpetually frozen soil plagued piping in all but the sunniest of southern exposures. Folks just took their empty cans along with them whenever they went into town, and filled them at the public spigot outside the grocery store. One result of this lack of plumbing was that no one cared much if your house was dirty, since everyone's house was dirty. That's the way it was. There was a laundry and shower house business over in Footprint, and a lot of folks went there once a week or so to get cleaned up. Tim and Kate had already gone down there three times in the past month. Their last showers had been just a few days back, so Kate was hoping they didn't smell too bad to go to the party and meet all the neighbors.

This was the day of Clem Curd's going away party! Everyone who lived on Round Top was invited. It was being given by his cousins, who lived five miles west of the place where the Goodmans and the Peters turned off to cross the decrepit bridge. If you were a moose you probably could have walked straight across the flat and been there in less than an hour; but by road it would be about eight sloppy miles. On that day the road was still drivable—barely. The recent downpours hadn't done it any good, though, and Tim guessed they'd soon have to start walking all the way down to Sleeping Moose.

Neil and Elsie were waiting for them when they got to their farm, and the four caravanned from there, with the old timers leading the way down their mudslide of a road to Curds' place.

When they arrived, there were already a handful of trucks and tractors parked out in the open space in front of the house. From the sounds that came out of it Kate guessed the party had been going on for quite a while. Tim parked the car's nose (and winch) facing out, in case the road got worse; and he and Kate hurried behind their guides through the rain and into the faded shake house as fast as possible. Time to meet the neighbors!

They entered through an arctic entryway that opened onto a fairly large room. All four walls were finished with plywood. The furnishings were pretty basic, just some wooden chairs and benches, and one large table. A closed door on the north side of the room probably led to the sleeping quarters. There was a Round Oak® wood stove at one end of the room and a kitchen with a wood cook stove on the other end. The big room was warm inside because both stoves were cooking.

The other partygoers took no notice of the arriving newcomers, since they were already well into their revelry. Boosted by some deceptively strong, colorless liquor called Everclear®, they were engaged in spirited conversations about everything from grizzlies to Congress. A door off the kitchen led to a pantry and everyone who came out of there had a full mug in his hand. Tim and Kate stood in the entryway, waiting to see if someone was going to welcome them, or what. No one did, so they finally edged into the din and made their way over to where the Goodmans had begun visiting with a man and woman who looked about Neil's age.

Kate looked at the worn curtains that framed each of the south facing windows. That detail made her wonder if there was a Mrs. Curd somewhere in the group. She saw only four women. Men outnumbered gals two to one at this party. That wasn't surprising, since Alaska was reputed to have ten men to every woman, even in Anchorage. Kate imagined a few good men would have managed to find themselves a woman before striking out into the bush, to live The Dream. But most of the men in this room looked like they didn't care so much about living The Dream, as that by living way out here they wouldn't have to put up with people. They'd probably gotten out of town just in time, before they'd up and killed somebody. Kate decided most of these fellows would never find a woman to put up with them. They looked dirtier than most, and their talk was crude. A woman among them would be like a lone heifer in a herd of bulls.

The Peters crossed over to the little knot of men and women crowded around the big wood stove. Elsie introduced them to the other three couples from the mountain. The older couple was named Myers. They were original homesteaders, too. Those four had known each other for years.

There was another, much younger couple sitting against the wall on the far side of the dining table.

Brian, who looked about Tim's age, squeezed around the table and went over to get a round of drinks for his new neighbors. Neil, who never drank alcohol, had already cornered Mr. Myers with the latest John Birch Society revelations.

Elsie and Mrs. Myers were talking baking; so Kate sat down and smiled at the other young woman in the room. The woman smiled back, and soon Kate confirmed that Anne and her husband Brian were the ones who lived at the vegetable garden and goats place with the beautiful view. Kate admired it every time they passed by on their way up or down the road to town. Good; one new friend for Kate, and maybe some playmates for their future children?

The last woman in the clutch was older than Kate, but she seemed cheery. Her name was Pat, and she wasn't Mrs. Curd. She was married to the old codger (her words) over there in the liquor room. Their place was back a piece, just this side of the turnoff to the bridge. Kate said she remembered seeing their house off in the trees on their way to the party.

Neil and Elsie were staying pretty busy talking to the pair they'd started with. Anne and Brian turned out to have a baby tucked in the corner behind the table, and most of their attention centered on their little papoose. Pretty soon Pat wandered off to mix with her husband and a short, wiry fellow who was complaining about a tree that had fallen across his access. Tim was drinking his Everclear and talking with Brian, so Kate looked for any other hints of a woman of the house. Except for those curtains, the place looked like it was being run by a pair of bachelors.

Besides the couples nearby there were five other men in the house. Elsie had pointed out both hosts, and the guest of honor; and she'd said that the wiry fellow was Jared. The last guy was huge, and he looked kind of feral. He had a sloping forehead that kind of reminded Kate of a bear. "And what's the last fellow's name?" she asked Elsie.

"That's Cliff. He keeps to himself. ...Lives down in the muskeg. Hunts."

Kate studied all five single men, knowing instantly that she'd rather die than be married to any one of these guys. ...To have to climb into bed with one of them. Ugh! The thought of it made her shiver. Her Tim was the handsomest man in the room; and Kate thought again how lucky she was!

She watched one of the two hosts, a big guy with greasy black hair wearing a red checked wool logger's shirt. He looked like he might've lived up there his whole life. Maybe born right there in that very house. The other brother came out of the pantry with a freshly refilled mug. He looked a lot like the first brother, only not as beefy. Same black hair: different checked shirt. Clearly brothers, though.

Clem wasn't built as big as his cousins, but he seemed to make up for that with an unnecessary meanness. He swaggered around from one fellow to the next, cursing and jabbing a finger into the listener's chest from time to time to make his point. Kate secretly thought it might be a blessing that he was moving away soon. She kept her head down and decided to stay away from 'cousin' Clem.

When Clement Curd felt it was time to make his parting speech, he strode over to the big stove. All five couples moved away, giving him a wide berth. He picked up an iron poker that stood leaning in the corner, and banged twice on the belly of the old stove to get everyone's attention. No one paid him any mind, and that didn't sit too well with his ego, so he banged again, harder. And *that* didn't sit too well with his cousins Greg and Craig.

"Hey, quit banging on the stove like that!" Greg shouted. "That was our ma's stove. You're liable to put a hole in it!" Meanwhile 'brother' Craig kept quiet, but he looked steamed.

"I'll quit bangin' when folks shut up for a minute so's I can say a few words here," Clem yelled back. Then he banged on the stove again, more to make his point, than to get folks' attention because by this time he already had pretty much everyone's attention.

"I told you to cut that out!" Greg yelled. He was getting sore, you could tell. That stove had probably been keeping the brothers warm since they were little scrub oaks.

But by now Clem was all stirred up, and he started beating on that fine antique pot belly like he was tryin' to kill it first, before it got him. He beat on it as hard as he could with the one hand, giving that iron beauty the thrashing of its life.

"You son of a bitch!" cousin Greg cursed. I told you to stop that!"

"You can kiss my ass!" Clem returned. Then he took an extra hard swing, and laid such a blow on that poor pot belly that it nearly shifted off its moorings. Now there was a big dent in the side of the heirloom.

"All right, that's it! You can just get goin' right now! Everybody out! This party's over!" Greg announced. Furious now, he started shoving his way toward his cousin. But the fellow who reminded Kate of a bear stepped up and held Greg back. Things looked like they might be getting out of hand.

"I ain't had my say, yet," Clem snarled, poker in hand.

"And I'm sayin' you're leaving! Now get out!!!"

"NOT 'TIL I'M READY...AND I AIN'T READY!" Clem hollered.

Greg started lunging toward his cousin with fists doubled. Clem dropped the poker, and bent down like he suddenly had a bad itch and was reaching to scratch his ankle.

Everyone who'd been in Sleeping Moose for any amount of time knew that Clem Curd kept a pistol in his boot. ...Something big was about to happen.

At the first sign of trouble, Craig Curd had started making his way over to the front door, so he'd be ready to grab the rifle off its hooks above if actions warranted. Now he was in place, and he reached for the loaded gun.

Greg shouted out to his brother, "Get 'im, Craig! He's goin' for his gun!"

That made Cliff let go of Greg's arm, and gallop out of the line of fire. It also made Clem turn to face Craig. The sneer on his face showed he was pretty sure he had the upper hand.

But Craig was ready for him, and Craig got his shot off first.

...Clem just stood there; didn't even blink. So Craig fired again.

Then, Clement Latrice Curd fell dead, right there in front of the belching stove.

As soon as the bangs and flashes started, everyone had hit the deck. Kate and Tim were down between the table and the wall, and they thought they should probably stay there for a while. But when Anne's baby woke up with a shrieking start, it got folks to breathing again and heads started popping back up all around the smoky room. Greg walked over and gave Clem's leg a kick. He was dead, alright.

When they were sure all the shooting was over, the rest of the celebrants started standing up and brushing off. Discussion was sparse, as everyone stared at the body of their prematurely, but not dearly, departed neighbor.

Greg Curd used the short-wave radio on the kitchen wall to transmit the news into town, and from there someone who had a telephone would forward the emergency call over to the State Troopers in Soldotna.

Cliff helped the Curd brothers carry their now deceased cousin Clem out the door and across the clearing to the ice house. Everyone else followed the grim procession out into the rain, and watched them lay the body on a palette and throw some ice and sawdust over it. Then, as quickly as they could do it without making their hosts any madder, the guests started giving excuses to get out of there and head for their trucks. Kate and Tim got into their rig without much in the way of goodbyes, and felt lucky to make it out of the clearing without another shot being fired.

"That was surreal. ...Did that really just happen?" Katie asked. She wasn't looking at Tim when she asked it. She was looking into the recent past, at the Wild West spectacle she had just witnessed.

"I guess there's a lot we don't know about living at the end of this road," was all Tim could think to say.

"Or about *who* is living at the end of this road," Kate added. "I'm sure glad they taught you how to shoot in the war. It looks like we might need some protecting up here, from time to time."

The rain was really smashing down now, and the road had turned to chocolate pudding.

They were both silent after that. Kate watched sheets of rain pour over the car's windows as they salamandered up the road toward Goodmans'.

***

Three days later, when the rains had let up enough so that a Trooper could finally get back in there to investigate, he wrote up Craig Curd's case as self-defense. Neil explained, "Everybody knew Clem kept a pistol in his boot and let his gun do most of his talking. He was just plain mean; didn't even want to *try* to get along with people." Kate guessed that was probably why he'd decided to leave the mountain: too many people.

The next week, after another terrific meal at Elsie's table, the four were talking over the bizarre events of that rainy night. Neil was saying, "I guess Craig is okay with the outcome. If he'd-a only shot *once*, the fine might o' been less than if he'd shot a moose out of season. But he shot twice. ...Darned pity, really. We was all glad to see Clem go. I think Craig did us a favor. ...Still, I reckon if I get any more invites over to Curds' for a get-together, I won't go. They take their going away parties a little too seriously for me."

***

The fall rains didn't slacken until the only artery into and out of town was totally useless. Whenever folks had to go for supplies, they now had to walk the road each way. Most of the vehicles Kate had seen at Curds' place were parked down at the turnoff in Sleeping Moose. Everyone was waiting for a hard freeze and a good snow. One fellow had already started using his snowmobile, splattering over the mud with little regard for the flat rubber tracks. But mostly, folks were walking.

As they hiked down toward their car one Sunday morning a week later, it dawned on Kate that they really were living on the Last Frontier. They had somehow settled down right where all the misfits mingled; and they were now the newest members of the "End of the Road" gang. Even if they had nothing else in common with those folks at Curds,' they all shared the same road. And a difficult road it was turning out to be.

September 30, 1976—Dear Mamasan,

More rain! I think it's rained every day this September. Our dirt road is nothing but bottomless ruts that are killers to drive in, and impossible to stay out of. We've had to start parking down at the turnoff, which means we walk six miles each way if we want to go anywhere. Needless to say, we don't go out much. I don't know if I should tell you this or not...But we were at a neighborhood party last week, and...

Kate recognized the couple who were walking up the road as she and Tim were walking down. "Look Tim. That's the Myers! They're the couple Elsie and Neil were talking to at the party. They're homesteaders, like the Goodmans."

When the four met up halfway between the bridge and the mushiest spot in the road, they stopped and reintroduced themselves. Charles and Augusta Myers said they had first homesteaded fifteen years back. They'd been working winters over across the inlet since the winter of '64-'65," Mr. Myers said. "Winters up here'll kill you, if one o' them Negroes don't. You might wanna' think about gettin' out o' here before long."

On the heels of the recent going away party, that sounded ominous. The Negroes? Kate frowned. "I don't remember seeing any Blacks around here."

"And it's best kept that way," Augusta Myers piped up. "That's the Mark of Cain on 'em, you know."

Before Kate could come up with a response, Tim changed the subject back to their annual exodus. "So you folks don't live here year around?"

"No. Not if we can help it. Getting out's the smartest way to survive the winters. And it's about the only way to make ends meet, too. Yep, most of us goes out in the late fall, and we come back in the spring."

It's nice here in the summer," Mrs. Myers said.

"Yes, indeed," Kate agreed to the good, neutral ground.

"So we're going up to say good-bye to Neil and Elsie. We're off to cook at the lumber camp for the winter," Augusta Myers said.

Kate thought Mrs. Myers looked tired, and maybe a little disenchanted after a lifetime on the mountain. She tried to cheer the woman up by saying, "We bought the back forty from Goodmans last summer. We're building a house up there."

"Oh." Mrs. Myers appeared to ponder that for a moment. "...Well, be prepared for things to take a lot longer than you think they're goin' to," she foreshadowed. "If you think it'll take you a year, then you better figure on ten."

"Oh, I think we'll be done quicker than that," Katie guessed. "Tim and I are both strong, and we won't need money for the first year, so we can work on it full time."

"So you're not plannin' on goin' outside this winter?"

"Well, we'll be using an outhouse this year, of course; but hopefully by this time next year we'll have our plumbing in."

Mrs. Myers raised an eyebrow, but said nothing. Their conversation at a stalemate, the four nodded their farewells. The two sourdoughs continued their trudge on up the hill to call on their friends; and the optimistic Cheechakos skipped off, focusing on a vision of unlimited opportunity.

"She seemed kind of negative, didn't she?" Kate reflected. Then she asked her mate for his honest reassurance. "You don't think it's going to take us ten years to build our house, do you?"

"Ten years? No way!" he pledged.

Call them dreamers. The pair continued their walk down over the river and through the woods. They would not be deterred.

***

That particular trip into Sleeping Moose had been more of a date than a major supply run. Bringing a big load home was going to be a lot easier in another week or two.

When they got into town they walked to the post office and got the mail, and then went around the corner of the aging log structure to a window where the postmaster's wife sold pizza by the slice. After a pleasant rest at the picnic table beside the store, they picked up a backpack's worth of groceries and filled two plastic cans half full with water from the spigot outside. Tim had suggested that it would be easier to carry a balanced load. And lighter too, if the cans weren't totally full. They were learning.

After that, they walked the long miles back up the mountain road. Then, it was corned beef hash, and off to bed!

"Maybe we should start collecting rain water," Kate said as she lowered the lantern wick. "If we use a clean pan it would be okay to drink, don't you think?"

"Um-hum," Tim murmured from his sleeping place alongside the wall.

Once she was in bed, Kate started thinking about Augusta Myers. Why had she said it would take ten years to get their house built? That was such a negative point of view.

***

"Tim, are you awake?"

"Mmmmmm." Not much movement from his side of the bed.

"It won't take us ten years to build our house, will it?"

He mumbled something like, "If anyonk do i' wuh can." And then he was out.

***

At three in the morning Kate tiptoed out through the big winter door. The day's drizzle had stopped, and the ground had turned crisp. Winter wasn't far away. She carefully navigated the freeze-stiffened ruts until she had cleared the corner of the cabin. Then she ducked, and squatted down under an alder. She didn't mind this ritual. In fact, she enjoyed it. On nights with a full moon and no wind, it could be other-worldly--especially if she happened to hear the crazy, cackling sound of a loon. Heaven on Earth, it was.

Kate peed; and when the hopeful call of a loon floated up through the emptiness from somewhere out on the marshy flat, she knew that the score for this arduous day had been evened.

CHAPTER 4
THE FIRST PRIVY STORY

If you've never had a privy, then you might think there's a lot of unnecessary outhouse humor in my mama's stories about life in the bush. But it's one of the necessities of life, and it has to be met head on. She used to say, "Sometimes it's so damned inconvenient that you might as well laugh about it." And when she told me, "We all share the same need for relief," I think she meant that both ways.

A.C.

As soon as that first surprise snow had melted, the new pioneers dug a hole big enough to last them until they got the house built and the plumbing in. They took turns digging. By lunchtime they had a sizable hole back in the trees behind Honeymoon Cottage. Time to rest and admire the new excavation. What a luxury to have a dedicated spot to go in! True, the seat and the actual walls might be a while in getting built, but until then, the move was do-able, if somewhat tricky.

Kate envisioned the maneuver. There was an alder sapling growing close to the edge of the pit. If you took hold of that, you would be able to swing your rear end out over the void. Yes sir, they were getting pretty fancy around there; practically ready for guests!

***

Their first visitor arrived a day or two after they had finished digging the big pit. Dick was Tim's longtime friend. He'd had to park his car between the bridge and the lake, and hike uphill through three miles of bear infested country, to see his friends' new place. No problem for this man, who was armed and loaded for bear, literally.

Dick was panting when he arrived at the little cabin. He stopped to catch his breath and admire the view for a minute, and then Tim showed him around inside Honeymoon Cottage. The whole tour took about ten seconds. Next, Katie showed Dick the exact spot where the moose had once slept, and indicated where the walls of their new log home would eventually go. Then Tim took Dick back down into the alder, to scope out the privy hole and line him out on the sapling handhold trick.

By then it was dusk, and the three crowded into the tiny lodge, where the two friends played serious cards and Kate rustled up her one-pot version of corned beef hash. (One can of corned beef, one onion stirred into instant potatoes, heat, add salt and pepper, and eat.) When the hash was hot, all three sat shoulder to shoulder on the edge of the sleeping platform and dined in the wavering lantern light.

After supper and a quick rinse of the pan and bowls, they talked, feeling protected under the breathy glow of the lantern. They talked about lots of stuff; those boyhood memories that the two men shared, and the opportunity that lay before this young married couple. Finally they hit upon Dick's favorite topic; the fact that a grizzly bear could be lurking in the immediate vicinity. The thought that a specimen of the family *Ursus Horribilis* might be right outside was both tantalizing and terrifying. Thus, the stories went on and on.

Finally they all decided it was time to turn in, so Dick asked for, and was handed a roll of toilet paper and a flashlight. His imagination afire with the evening's tales of wild beast attacks, he opted to take his revolver along with the two necessities. Tim opened the door of the cabin and aimed his friend in the direction of the distant black hole.

As Dick waded out into darkness, Kate (who had been clever enough to visit the pit in daylight) darted out the door and peed under the stars. Gorgeous! She was back inside and into her flannel nightgown long before Dick got back.

Since they'd all be sleeping in the one bed, Kate and Tim sat on the edge of the platform, waiting for Dick to return so they could get into bed in the right order. Kate needed the outside, since she made the most midnight runs.

"Dick's been gone a long time," she said finally. What do you think he's doing out there?"

"I don't know, but if he's not back in two minutes I'll go fish him out," Tim said.

A minute later they heard the sound of hasty footsteps crushing fallen leaves. The door burst open, and Dick bolted inside and slammed the door shut. Tim jumped up, ready to reach for the shotgun. "Is there something out there?"

"I think so. I'm not sure. ...Maybe."

The three froze to listen for a few seconds. When they were sure that there was nothing prowling around outside, Dick started telling them what had happened.

"The whole time I was out there I kept thinking about grizzly bears. I had the flashlight and toilet paper in one hand, and my gun in the other. When I got to the part about holding onto the alder branch, it took me a while to decide what to give up."

"Which one did you finally let go of?" Tim was finding it hard to keep a serious face.

"Well, I'll tell you this," Dick confided. "I never let go of my gun!"

***

Right after Dick's visit they really got to work on that long-overdue outhouse.

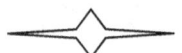

But it was still inconvenient at times

CHAPTER 5
COALING, EATING, TALKING

A couple of weeks later, when the road hardened up Neil and Elsie took Tim and Kate out on their first coaling expedition. The old-timers made it sound easy. "You just wait until there's a storm from the right direction, drive out west of Kenai, wait by the pier until the tide is out, drive through the slough the minute it's shallow enough, pick up all the coal you can before the tide starts coming back in, and take it home."

With the Goodmans supervising that first coal run, it did seem like a pretty slick way to heat your house. After they'd dropped their black bounty beside the door of Honeymoon Cottage, Neil invited the two down for supper, which was a perfect way to end the day.

After a meal of lamb, squash, kale, and more home-canned tomatoes, biscuits and honey, Elsie brought out wild blueberries with cream and put a kettle on for coffee or tea.

Neil finished off his meal with a handful of Rolaids, and Elsie set out four mugs for the final course of the evening. Then she filled another kettle to heat water for dishes. During the lull while they were waiting for the water to heat, all four rested heavy elbows on the table, digesting and chewing over the latest news from the neighborhood.

"Yup," Neil said, as if he'd been thinking about the story for a few minutes. "I reckon Snyder must have been pretty surprised when the Myers showed up a few days earlier than expected."

"Oh. We met the Myers last week," Kate said. "They were walking up the road when we were walking down."

"That's right. They finally got headed back to Jakalof for the winter." Neil sounded happy for them. "They told us they'd had quite a time finding a new caretaker for their place. Said they wouldn't take Fram back, even if he swore he wouldn't never again do what he done last spring."

"Fram?" That was a name Kate hadn't heard before. "Was he at Curds' party?"

"Nope. He's away to Utah. ...Went there when Charlie Myers kicked him out last spring. You gotta' understand," Neil seemed to feel that some explaining was needed; "Frampton Snyder, he's kind of strange. ...Some say he was kicked in the head by a horse, but I don't know for sure. Anyway, he don't have a place of his own, you see, so Charlie Myers had him to stay at their place while they were gone, to tend the animals, and such..." Neil paused, as if lost in thought.

"Go ahead and tell 'em what happened, Neil. They're waiting," Elsie prompted, "and the kettle's steaming."

That got the reminiscing cowboy going again. "Anyhow, when the Myers showed up just a little ahead of schedule, they found two calves in the kitchen and a litter of pigs in their bed!"

"Pigs?" Both the Peters were surprised.

"Yes sir. That's so. Fram said he was, 'just keeping 'em warm, that's all.' But o' course Myers kicked 'im out right away. He said he didn't take kindly to no pigs in his blankets. That's when Fram took off down to Utah, and we haven't heard hide nor hair of him since."

"But he'll be back one day, more than likely," Elsie said, finishing up the modern folktale. "There ain't many places would put up with him." She pushed her steel chair away from the table and went to fetch the hot dishwater.

"I'll never be able to think of 'pigs in a blanket' the same way again," Kate said with a half laugh, as she got up to help Elsie. "Let's just hope he finds a place down in Utah that suits him. I don't need to see any more Clem types on the mountain."

"Oh don't worry," Neil said. "He ain't violent. He's just kinda' simple, you might say. But you can bet that there'll be another troublemaker to come along. As soon as one leaves, another one just shows up to take his place. That's the type likes to settle at the end of the road. Less people around; less people to have to shoot, I expect." Sadly, Neil Goodman didn't really look like he was joking.

While Elsie poured boiling water into the dishpan, Kate cleared all the dishes from the table, and then stood shoulder to shoulder with Elsie to help wash up the mess from supper. True to tradition, the women washed the dishes while the men discussed politics. That's the way things were back then on the Last Frontier.

On this particular night, Neil went into great detail about the Rockefellers and their Tri-Lateral Commission conspiracy. His analysis of the nation in peril through the stealthy takeover and establishment of a new World Government lasted until after midnight. Finally, the Peters went home to their cabin, and Elsie could get to sleep. Yes. She would really love that two room house, if she ever got it. Kate was pretty sure.

***

One night, the storm they'd been waiting for moved in and started pounding the region.

"We'll be coaling in the morning," Tim predicted.

Before dawn they grabbed two empty five gallon buckets and drove the fifty miles over to Kenai. They parked beside the last pier, and waited for the tide to go out.

"...I think the slough's just about low enough," Tim said at last. They'd been waiting there for about forty-five minutes, and they'd watched the sea recede almost magically from the tall pilings.

"Let's go for it." He drove straight across the draining ribbon of seawater to the outer beach, where numerous lumps of sea-soaked coal lay half buried in the wet sand. There it was, free for the taking. As the waves continued to ebb, more and more shiny black bumps popped up out of the waterlogged beach. It came in chunks sized from grapefruits to wheel rims. The big ones might last longer, but the littler ones were a lot easier to pull loose, and fit into the stove. The two worked hard and fast, pulling the chunks free with a sucking pop, and slinging bucket after heavy bucket of coal into the back of their Toyota. By the time their load of coal reached the car's windows, the tide was already starting to come back in.

"We'd better get out of here now," Kate said. "The tide's coming in."

"I think we still have time to get a few more pieces. See all those big ones over there by the water?"

"Please Tim. It looks really soft down there, and I don't want to swamp the car."

"Okay. Okay. Get in. It would be bad to watch the car float away up Cook Inlet."

"And if it got caught in the outgoing tide, it wouldn't stop 'til it reached Korea," Kate added.

They tossed their empty buckets on top of the load and got into the car. By the time they got back to the slough, crossing it looked scarier than ever.

"I think it's even higher than before. Do we dare?"

"We have to go, or this car'll be headed back to Asia." He put the 4x4 in gear, and burst out into and across the rapidly swelling stream. Kate held onto the dash and unconsciously lifted her feet. She hoped they'd make it across, but she was ready to wade for it if their luck ran out. Tim did a masterful job piloting the craft across the strait to safety.

"That was hairy," Kate said when they were back on solid ground.

"Hairy?" Tim sounded surprised. "No. That was fun!"

They decided to grab some breakfast before heading home. Looking and feeling like real locals, they strolled into the Bait Café, nonchalantly leaving their load of coal out front in plain view. After pancakes, ham and eggs, hash browns, toast and coffee, they were ready to go.

They made one more stop, half way between Footprint and Sleeping Moose, because they got a flat tire.

This unhappy turn of events necessitated emptying the entire load of coal out onto the side of the road, so Tim could get to the jack. Then they loaded every last piece of coal back into the car and continued the trek home. By the time they reached Sleeping Moose it was nearly dark, and the end of a long, long day.

The pair bumped over every frozen rut that road had ever generated all the way up to Honeymoon Cottage, and added the new coal to the pile under the tarp. Kate was disappointed that their stockpile of fuel still looked pretty puny. Free fuel: You haul away. Hah! True, the price was right, but at what cost? And besides, she didn't really like the smell it gave off when it burned. Wood smoke reminded her of the family camping trips, when she was a girl. Saltwater soaked coal smelled like something recently freed from far beneath the earth.

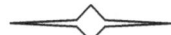

"Will you tell me some more about riding the range?" The two women were standing in Elsie's kitchen, making biscuits. Elsie had a lot of great stories to tell about growing up as a cowgirl in Arizona. Her parents had no sons, but she and her three sisters helped their dad round up strays right along with the hired hands.

"Did you ever come across a rattlesnake out there?" Kate asked.

The aging cowgirl paused, put down her baking sheet and looked back across half a century. "Oh, I guess I musta' killed two or three of 'em...a day."

Kate caught her breath. "You killed two or three rattlesnakes *a day*?"

"Yup, probably." Elsie was talking low and slow, as always.

Good grief! "Well, did you shoot 'em, or what?"

"Oh no, my daddy wouldn't let me have a gun. I just used my reins, or spurs, or whatever was handy." She slid the biscuits into the oven, and then picked up a boiling hot potato which she started peeling with her bare hands. No doubt about it, that Elsie was *some* woman. Kate absolutely loved her!

After another fantastic meal with the Goodmans, Neil and Tim sat and discussed politics while the women stood side-by-side at the sink and washed the dishes. That's when Kate finally gumptioned-up the nerve to ask Elsie something she'd been wondering since the day they met. "Elsie, are you part Indian?"

"Heavens, no. What makes you ask that?"

"Your hair; it's so black, and you don't have any gray hair at all."

Elsie laughed. "Why, honey, that's from a bottle!"

Kate was stumped. "Really?"

"Sure. I've got enough gray up there to braid a rope to China," Elsie said.

"You continue to amaze me, Elsie," was all Katie said.

"Well I just want to look nice without takin' time out for it," Elsie said. ...O' course I tried gussying up once or twice, before I learned better. Around here there's mostly just enough time to get the chores done and not much left over."

Elsie told Kate about the day she and Neil cleared the north field, which the Peters now called home. "Neil had a little tractor that he drove up and down that sloping field, while I walked along behind the tractor picking up all the sticks that the plow had turned. I made piles of them up at all four edges of the field. That was a hot and dusty morning," she recalled. "Finally, at noon we walked back home to rustle up dinner. After we ate, Neil rested up in his recliner for a bit, while I hauled and heated water and washed all the dishes. ... I guess I shoulda' go-mollied 'em that time... So anyway, just when I'd finished cleaning up and was fixin' to sit down and rest for a minute, Neil jumps up and tells me he reckons it's time we got back to work. And so we did."

She'd told the tale simply, without any hint of complaint. In fact, she almost said it with a laugh. …Yup. She'd pulled her own weight around there all those years. That was for sure.

Kate thought about what it meant to be a pioneer's wife. Did she have what it took to fill boots as impressive as Elsie's? Was she as strong and perseverant? Tim had always treated her like an equal. But still, after those rosy days of college in the Sixties, this was a very different land, and a very different era she had come to. This place was still the frontier.

Could she fit into the traditional woman's role, when necessary? She hoped so. In the past, she'd usually been able to rise (or lower) to whatever standards the occasion called for. One thing was for sure; both Elsie and Neil were genuine "Salt-of-the-Earth" folks. You wouldn't meet finer bush mentors anywhere!

CHAPTER 6
WOLF TRACKS BEHIND THE CABIN

When the tomatoes in Elsie's coal-heated hothouse kicked the bucket one frosty night, and berry gorged grizzlies started heading for their favorite riverside fishing holes, it looked like fall was in full swing. Within a few days, several layers of snow had drifted in, smoothing out Round Top's domed brow until it looked like a huge pillow at the head of their private forty acre bed.

***

Nov. 20, 1976, Dear Mamasan,

Winter's here. A wet autumn has been shoved aside. Now Tim and I sit together as long as it's light, and then we hit the sack right after the sun sets. It's best to be under the covers before the place cools off. Tim likes to make us cozy by filling the stove with big chunks of beach coal right at the last. But then--when it takes off and the cabin gets hot--he jumps up and starts shoveling the whole shootin' works out into the snow ! Then it gets cold again. I wish he would just put in less coal, or maybe open the cabin door for a few minutes. But I remember what you said about picking my battles. So I just *watch him do it his way. Still, it seems so wasteful, with everything being so hard to get up here.*

Fall moved away, and winter came to stay.

One night, shortly before the coal ritual, they heard a strange noise coming from outside. It was just a low buzz at first; but it got louder and louder, and it was definitely coming closer...

"It's the Goodmans on snowmobiles!" Tim sounded the all clear as soon as he'd popped his head out the door and recognized their neighbors.

"Howdy," Neil called out. "We're on our way up to the top of the mountain. It's a perfect night, still and clear. We thought you two might want to come along."

"...On a snowmobile? Sure! Yes. You bet! Can you wait a minute while we put on our gear?"

Tim and Kate didn't have insulated snowmobiling suits like the ones the Goodmans had on, so they donned the warmest gear they owned: insulated Carhartts, Sorrels, L.L. Bean® moose-hide mittens, scarves and wool knit hats with ear flaps. When they were all zipped up they went outside, closed the cabin latch securely, and walked over to admire the unfamiliar machines. Both rigs looked ancient, like relics from the first crop of snowmobiles ever produced. Their weathered yellow noses were chipped and beaten, and Elsie's rig had a Bungee® cord holding the seat in place. The machine Neil sat on was wider, and it had two black rubber tracks and one ski where Elsie's machine had just the opposite.

"This one here is a double track. You and Kate can take it, and we'll drive the single track. ...Oh, and we call 'em 'snowmachines' in Alaska," Neil corrected, "because we work 'em hard up here. 'Snowmobiles' is what they ride around to play on down in the Lower Forty-Eight,"

Neil dismounted and demonstrated the throttle and the pull-start to Timothy. After Tim had gotten the hang of the starter rope, the mentor walked over and climbed onto the single track snowmachine and sat down in front of Elsie. They were ready to go.

Tim gave the rope a good pull, and when the crusty trooper started right up he stepped onto the running board, swung his leg over the seat, sat down and took hold of both handles. Kate had been looking at the whittled wooden stopper that stuck out of the double track's gas tank. Was that safe? ...But then she climbed onto the bench seat right behind Tim, and wrapped her arms around his waist. "Tally–ho!" she cried, and the convoy departed from the station.

The Goodmans led, and the Peters followed, and the two machines ran on the bear trail all the way through the windbreak. Ducking under branches and leaning into turns, Kate found it more like riding a motorcycle than a horse. But it wasn't scary. It was fun! When they swished out past the last of the trees and broke free on the far side, they saw no sign of human habitation at all, just stars and snow. The machines were zipping across a wide, slanting meadow that led up to the ridgeline. Kate threw her head back to witness the untainted sky above them. "What a ride!" she shouted to anyone, and to no one. Ahead, their path to the summit was faintly illuminated by the two antique headlights. Above them lay an endless spray of stars.

Bounding up the ridge they reached the domed top, and everyone got off to stand and share in the gloriousness of this mountaintop experience. They were now on the highest point around, where no trees, or brush, or snow collected against the ever-present wind. Looking southwest toward Sleeping Moose they could see two luminous arms, stretching out to greet the highway as it passed through town. And directly east Kate thought she could see a light. Was that the other homestead, way across the flat? "Is that Myers' place" she asked Elsie.

"Yup. That's right." Then Elsie turned and pointed out the silhouettes of two small, dark lumps barely visible in the starlight. "That's your house down there. And that one out past the woods and over to the left of the flat field, that's our place."

Kate's eyes traveled northward from the two homes. In that direction, there were no lights at all.

"We might be the only people around for miles," Tim said, voicing their common awe.

Neil spoke to that. "We may be the only *people*, but there's lots of black bear and wolves to keep us company out here."

Both Cheechakos took a quick look to the sides and behind them. They really were vulnerable out there, all alone with whatever meat eaters might be watching. Kate searched the darkness for staring eyes, and hoped she wouldn't find any.

The four spent a few more minutes on that wonderful, powerful spot, and then *whoosh!* Down the mountain they went, sweeping back over the same trail they'd carved on the way up. Both snowmachines were aimed straight for the hand-hewn refuge that waited for them, promising safety and warmth at the extreme upper edge of civilization. When they got to the open field Tim knew the way home from there. He increased the gas and steered over to the left to ride beside the Goodmans.

...And that's when the snowmachine stopped in its tracks.

"What happened?" Kate asked, astonished.

"I'm not sure. It just conked out." Tim sounded as confounded as she.

They both stepped off the machine into nearly waist-deep snow, to stare at the thing. Kate felt as helpless as a teamster whose overloaded mule just died.

"Are you two having trouble?" Neil asked, after he'd circled back to see why half the party had quit.

"I don't know what happened," Tim shrugged. "It just died." He had already started fumbling at the frozen latches, trying to get the hood open.

"No need to lift the cowling," Neil said. He pointed to the last weaving track the machine had carved into the snow, where Tim had pulled out to the left. "See that? You got off the packed trail right there. She's bogged down in the snow, that's all. Got ice packed in the tracks. Here. We'll just roll 'er over on her side; and let's get them things cleared out."

The two pioneer women stood and watched as the two pioneer men rolled the ailing machine up onto its side and began doctoring it.

"Hey look-y there," Neil said, stopping his chipping long enough to point to a set of animal tracks that crossed over the trail about ten feet from where they worked. The tracks went down into a drifting swale to the east. "That there is a wolf track," he said. "See the dragging toenail in the center? ...Probably a family of 'em standing over in that gully right now, listening to us. You two care to go take a look?"

"No thanks." Kate answered pretty fast.

The men pounded and chipped away at the frozen snow that had wedged in between the tracks and their rollers. After a few minutes the machine's belly was cleared, and they righted it again.

Then they were off, dashing through the dark, hurtling over hummocks and winding through the woods. Finally, they arrived at sweet little Honeymoon Cottage. Home safe!

By now everyone was ready for some cocoa and conversation. Neil and Elsie squeezed in beside Tim on the bed; and Katie pumped up the Coleman stove and made cocoa. Then the three shuffled over again, so she could join them. That night's conversation centered on wolves. Neil said they hadn't ever given him any trouble, but Elsie said she'd never met a wolf she completely trusted.

After the Goodmans left, Tim stoked the fire and loaded it up with coal. Then, he and his adoring wife climbed into bed together.

***

Kate awakened a couple of hours later, as Tim was climbing over her to tend the stove. She watched with one eye, as he started throwing all of their precious red-hot coals out into the hissing snow.

December 2, 1976 – Dear Mamasan,

Last night we rode on snowmachines up to the top of Round Top Mountain—and we crossed paths with a pack of wolves! Don't worry--both parties are fine.

CHAPTER 7
THE ROAD TO SPRING

December 14, 1976 – Dear Mamasan,

Our road is disintegrating under all this snow. We're thinking of heading out for the rest of the winter. Then we can return in the spring, just like the geese. That's what people up here do. Tim hopes to go out of the Laborer's Hall, and I'll try the Culinary Union. If we can both get pipeline jobs, we'll have plenty of money come spring.

Tim went out right away, headed for Franklin Bluffs. Kate, whose number wasn't as good as his, didn't fare as well. She got a temporary assignment out to Pump Station #1, but it only lasted two weeks. Then she ended up staying in Anchorage at Tim's friend Dick's place, sleeping on a quilt on his living room floor and working as a teacher's assistant for the remainder of the term. It was okay. She spent her evenings drawing house plans and her weekends cruising garage sales. She found a lot of good, used household items, and stored them in Dick's carport until the spring.

Tim called when he could, which wasn't often. The phone lines from the camps were choked. It seemed that *everyone* had left someone behind.

February 13, 1977 – Dear Mamasan,

I miss Tim so much. I don't like to think of us spending every winter apart for the rest of our lives. It may be the way they do it in the bush, but it's no way to stay married.

***

April 3, 1977 – Dear Mamasan,

I've been fine, thanks, keeping busy. Tim was here for ten days of R&R, but he just left. This winter is passing much too slowly. We can't wait for spring to get here. Tim plans to hold onto his job until June. By then our road should be good and hard. Just two more months, and then we're headed back to our promised land.

***

June finally came. Tim quit his job, and they packed all of Kate's garage sale bargains in the car and a used snowmachine trailer she'd bought, and made a beeline to the mountain. They had just about everything they'd need to set up house, *including* an old kitchen sink unit.

Those original Okies couldn't have driven with any more determination than Tim and Kate Peters did on the day they hauled that load around inlet curves and between glaciered mountains, anxious to get to the place they called "home."

As they drove down out of the Chugach Mountains, they stopped to celebrate with an ice cream cone in Windsor Landing. After that they really started to get excited and those last few miles flew by.

***

"...Damn it! Why is this road still muddy?" Kate demanded, expecting an answer from no one. She was standing with hands on hips, staring up the six mile long, mostly impassible driveway that ended at her door. "It's the middle of June! Breakup should be over by now. This road should be dry! Damn it!"

Tim had pulled the car and trailer off the highway; and Kate had walked up the road a few feet to see how hard the mud was.

Tim eased the loaded vehicle up beside her. "It still looks pretty soft. I guess at this elevation breakup starts later, and takes longer."

"...Longer than a month?"

"Apparently," he said.

"Do you think we can get in if we use the winch?"

"Not if it gets any worse up ahead, which it most likely will."

Kate pictured the always-boggy "lake" section that lay just past the bridge. In her vision, she saw the road grader stuck along the wayside; a perennial reminder of the difficulties of their road home.

"Looks like we won't be driving home today," Tim said.

Kate nodded, and then looked over at their packed car and trailer. "But what'll we do with all this stuff? We can't just leave it here."

"If we can get it far enough off the highway, I doubt anyone will bother it. We'll take it in as far as we can and just park it 'til the road's dry."

"Which will hopefully be sometime this summer," Kate said, exhaling a whiff of sarcasm.

Their plan set, they crossed the highway to pick up all the mail that had accumulated in their long absence. There was a letter from Elsie saying that they had headed out to the fishing camp in Katmai. They would be back soon.

This was an interesting bit of news. It meant that, until the homesteaders returned, Tim and Kate would be the only ones living up past the bridge. They got back into the land cruiser; and Tim used low gear to fishtail the long load up the road as far as they could go. They got almost as far as the bridge, where regrettably, they came to a stop.

"We'd better park here," Tim said. "If we go across the creek, we might not be able to turn around anywhere when we want to get back into town."

"True. Backing out over the bridge wouldn't be easy. Looks like we're walking from here," Kate said.

She got out, and started assessing what items absolutely *had* to come with them and what could stay behind.

In the end, they decided to leave everything behind except one can of water, which they now toted between them. It was a struggle.

They hadn't covered much ground before Tim made a suggestion. "We'd better start thinking about how we're gonna' get water during breakup. This won't work, carrying it up from here."

"Agreed," said Kate, already panting.

"I think we should try to dig out that spring Neil showed us last year," he said.

"Sounds like a good plan to me." Kate said, taking the opportunity to set down her half of the heavy can.

Tim matched her move, and they stretched and rested for a moment. "...How about first thing tomorrow?"

"Fine with me. And since we'll be getting fresh spring water in the morning, can we dump some of this out? No point in carrying five gallons uphill, if we don't have to."

Tim had no argument with her suggestion, so they tipped the can and poured out half of the precious drink. That lightened their load significantly, and they made it up the mountain in less than an hour, even though the "lake" section owned up to its name. They ran the gauntlet of the bog, slipping through boot-high mud and jumping around puddles that were deeper than their knees.

Then, as the road started to climb up out of the flat they got a better pace going. Kate was able to keep up with Tim pretty well because she now had a song going in her head, fostering her enthusiasm. She remembered that when she was a little girl, her mamasan always kept them singing on those treks through Haleakala Crater. So she sang: "I love to go a-wandering along the mountain track. And as I go I love to sing, my knapsack on my back." That tune had a great rhythm for hiking up mountains.

They hiked right past the empty homesteaders' hut: no one there. They crossed the big flat field and followed the access road down into the woods beyond. These trees were the last buffer between their world and the rest of the world. When they cleared the last spruce, their elegant front yard blossomed in full color ahead of them.

"Look! It's Honeymoon Cottage!" Kate cried. "I saw it first, so I get a kiss!"

"There it is," Tim said, giving his bride her requested reward. "The place looks good, don't you think?"

"Wonderful! Beautiful! Gorgeous!" Kate sounded satisfied.

They hastened a clip. They were almost home. A thousand indigo lupines nodded at them as the two wove between the clusters of waist-high plumes. "Look at all these flowers, Tim!" Kate was giddy. "Oh hello! Hello you darling, beautiful flowers! And hello, you darling, beautiful house! I've missed you so much!"

At last they stood at their Honeymoon Cottage. Kate relinquished her half of the can of water to Tim, and he swung it up onto the shelf outside the door. A gentle afternoon breeze cooled the tired hikers as it wafted across their private alpine meadow. Then Tim stepped forward and opened the padlock that had been protecting their home.

Kate was given the honor of actually opening the door; and when she did, a flood of late afternoon sunshine poured inside, saturating the cabin with amber light. Tim made a quick inspection of the place. The floor looked dry, and there were no signs of visiting varmints.

"Good. We're home!"

Katie stepped in behind Tim. "Gosh, I'd forgotten how small this place is. ...But I love every square inch of it!" She wanted to spread her arms with joy, but thought better of it.

It didn't take long for them to pick up where they'd left off. Tim pumped up both the stove and the lantern, and Kate found some left-over canned corned beef and dehydrated mashed potatoes on the kitchen shelf. She cooked up her specialty, and felt happy to be home.

They ate supper outside, sitting on stumps, eating hash and admiring the alpenglow on the far landscape. How wonderful to be right there in front of their very own little handmade honeymoon house! And the view wasn't bad, either.

***

The sun popped up over the hill at around four the next morning, and Kate trotted out to pee. Then she took a moment to say hello to everything out there. Tim emerged a minute later, stepped over to the side of the cabin and stood scratching his stomach and squinting at the new red sun, while Katie ducked back inside and grabbed the speckled blue coffee pot.

"Would you like some coffee?"

Tim grunted once, which usually meant 'yes,' so she measured out four cups of the liquid gold they had carried up from the car, and set it on the Coleman. As she pumped up the propane stove she thought about how they would probably have a can filled with fresh spring water by evening. Why not use two more cups and make oatmeal?

After breakfast they went off to locate the source of their spring. Katie carried the shovel. Tim carried the shotgun. Dropping down over the side of their hill, they quickly found themselves fighting taller-than-usual grass. Taking this as a clear sign that there must be a source of water nearby, they fought every chest-high jungle step happily. Kate was relieved that there were no snakes in the forty-ninth state. "I guess it's too cold up here for snakes," she reasoned.

"Winters would do them in. All we have to worry about in this grass is the occasional bad-tempered bear," her protector said with a grin. "...And by the way, you'll need to learn how to use this shotgun soon."

Kate tisked at that, and said, "Maybe someday."

Neil had told them there were black bears around all year long. He'd said the grizzlies spent winters fishing on the lakes and rivers, and summers browsing for berries up behind the mountain. "The quickest route from salmon patch to berry patch runs right through your place," he had said.

Tim nodded. "Since it's spring I guess we should be on the lookout for migrating grizzlies. But we don't need to worry too much," he added a second later. "These valleys are black bear territory, not grizzly. The grizzlies will all be up on the road."

"Why is that?"

Tim took a guess. "Easier walking?"

When the pair pinpointed some seepage beneath an extra-large spruce tree, Tim traded in the shotgun for the shovel and started digging. After ten minutes they switched tools, and Kate dug. They alternated until midday, when they finally stopped digging and sat resting beside their new catch basin. The plan was to put a plywood dam across the lower end, with a shallow channel chiseled out at the top, so the pool could continually rejuvenate. Kate thought it was a good design; no moving parts to break.

Satisfied so far, they hiked back up to the cabin to get peanut butter and jelly sandwiches, and the quarter sheet of plywood left over from their privy construction. Feeling confident that victory was close at hand, they used up the last of the water on some powdered lemonade and then walked back down toward the spring. Tim carried the plywood and Kate carried the empty water can, which would soon be full again. They dropped down into the tall grass, and she started humming in case there were any bears around.

Tim set the slab of wood on its edge at the low end of the pool, and together they pressed it down deep into the mud. Next they gathered rocks and stacked them up against the wood on either side, to help hold it in place. Then the project was done!

It looked just like a dam.

"If this spring has a decent flow, the pool should be full by tomorrow," Tim predicted.

Katie stared at the recently unearthed sediment as it swirled around in the catchment pond. "Do you think it'll settle out? Look at all that silt."

"It should be okay, as long as nothing disturbs it. Just be careful when you fill the cans, that's all. We'll have to get a ladle. Anyway, this water's fresher than anything you'll get out of a spigot in town."

Before they went home that evening, Tim laid the open can down on its side; and they both sat down to watch the languid liquid as it tried to detour around, but was eventually sucked down into the vacuum of the empty can. They would have water in the morning.

"This first can full of water might taste pretty earthy," Kate thought to herself. But she was ecstatic, never the less.

CHAPTER 8
FAIR PLAY

June 16, 1977—Happy Birthday Mamasan!

Thanks for the offer, but it looks like we won't be needing a generator, after all. Rural Electric says we should have power by July--which is two months later than they originally told us, but it'll still be in time for mixing the cement and all. We'll be starting the new house very soon! After we get the basement finished we'll move in there and begin working on the upstairs. We should have the whole thing done by this time next year. This is really the beginning--and I'm <u>thrilled</u>!

These were intoxicating days for Tim and Kate. Their whole extended honeymoon was perfect, especially now that it was summer and they were just burning wood. The smell of wood smoke permeated their clothing and their hair, and Katie loved to smell it on her man.

June 29 1977—Dear Mamasan,

The road has finally hardened up and it's navigable again, as long as you can survive the ruts. Our trusty little tank is able to carry us all the way home, and we're parking right beside the cabin! Our neighbors, the Goodmans are back now too. They went out to work, just like the rest of us. But we're all back home now. It's shaping up to be a perfect summer.

"Let's drive up to the summit today." Tim came up with the idea as they sat on their stumps outside, sipping coffee and admiring the morning light. Purple and yellow flowers stretched fingertips up to the sunshine, carpeting the meadow all the way to the drop off by the spring. It was divine.

"The ground is hard enough to get up there now, and we deserve a day off," he continued.

"Okay, I'm game if you are," Katie agreed, wondering what kind of flowers they'd see growing up there.

After their usual bowl of mush with raisins, they saddled up and headed out to tackle the wilderness that began right behind their cabin.

Tim figured they would make it up to the summit and be back in time for lunch.

The pair had been working like slaves, preparing for the start of construction on their masterpiece. They'd calculated the number of cinder blocks they would need to build the basement, and figured it would be more than a thousand. So far they had bumped up the road with six loads of fifty each. Those three hundred blocks were stacked beside their proposed site, right where the moose had once slept. Navigating the road was still tough, though. Maybe it would smooth out after a few more trips, or maybe Neil would use the dozer, or they could hook up that old wooden road grader and help it along. They would bring up the rest of the blocks then. In the meantime, it was a lovely summer day and they were in a beautiful spot. What was there to complain about?

It was fun bouncing along like safari travelers, carving their own way through the underbrush. After the bush rig had plowed its way through an alder border at the top edge of the field Neil and Elsie had cleared, they entered the stand of spruce that would one day protect their house from the north wind.

Out the other side of that windbreak the adventurers burst into wide open sunshine. From the base of this field, their route was a pretty straight incline through a bunch of mounded dead grass and then up the rounded ridgeline, all the way to the top. Katie recognized the spot where they had encountered wolf tracks the winter before. They would be crossing right over it.

Their little Japanese tank charged into the expanse of grassy bumps and traveled about two hundred feet. Then the car came to a curious stop. The engine was still running, and Tim gunned it, but the moveable fortress refused to move.

"Is there something about this particular spot?" Kate half joked.

Tim's only response was an order. "Get out, and when I give it gas, tell me what you see," he said to his partner.

Kate climbed out of the car and took a look to see what was holding them up. When Tim accelerated, the little tank's wheels turned just fine, but they were spinning in air. The car was stuck on top of a giant lump of dead grass, flailing like an impaled bug. "We're stuck on a hummock," she reported back.

Apparently they had just encountered that infamous foe to man and machine, the organic obstacle that festered all over the Alaskan backlands, the bane of the bush that thwarted ease of passage to all but wolves, bear and moose. Kate knew them as hummocks, but the locals called them "nigger heads."

"Let's use the winch," Tim said, as he got down out of the driver's seat and went around to the front bumper. The plan was for Kate to run the mechanism, while Tim walked the cable out and hooked it around the nearest sturdy anchor. He began loosening the cable, but soon stopped and looked around. He waggled the loose end of the winch cable but saw nothing to hook it to. "I don't think we can reach any of those trees back behind us," he called out, after estimating the distance and the angle. "Do you see anything up the hill that we could use?"

Kate looked up ahead. "We're above the tree line, so we'll have to look for a big rock or something I guess." She waded through the hummocks, looking for an anchor that would be even more immovable than their heavy green tank. Once again, she was glad there were no snakes. ...But bears were a real possibility.

Tim threw open the back doors and started rummaging around, tossing shovels and jumper cables out onto the grass. Eventually he located the small jack that had come with the car, and jammed it in place under the frame. He fitted the miniature parts together and started to pump the thin, jointed steel arm. On the second pump, the undersized base sank straight down into the ground. "Damn it!"

He spat, pumped some more, and still made no headway. The jack was useless.

Kate returned from her fruitless search, and saw that her husband was getting frustrated. She stood out of the way, reported her findings, and awaited further instructions.

"I think we're in some trouble here," Tim admitted. "We need to go back to the cabin and get something to put under this stupid jack base."

"Like what?"

"Something big and flat... I think the G.I. stove lid might work." Tim looked up at the mountain, on the other side of which lay twenty thousand, zillion square miles of wilderness. "I wish I'd brought the shotgun," he muttered.

There probably *were* grizzlies migrating through there right about now. "It's okay," Kate offered; her turn to be the hero. "I can sing, and they'll get out of our way."

Tim grunted, picked up one section of the Japanese jack handle for protection, and the pair started walking down the hill, back toward the woods they had just come through. As soon as they got close to the trees, Katie began singing at full volume. It was a quickstep version of the aria from

Carmen. For some reason, that was the song that popped into her head.

"Easy there!" Tim said. "You don't want to piss 'em off."

"I just want to give any bears fair warning," Kate said. But she lowered her voice in deference to her partner's wishes, and started singing the chorus of the hiking song instead. Finally their sweet little Honeymoon Cottage stood just ahead of them in plain view, and not a bear in sight.

Half an hour later they were climbing back up to the car, toting jack handle, stove lid and gun.

It turned out that the flat metal stove lid didn't do the trick either, so they hiked back down, *again.* This time they marched in silence, since Tim was out of patience and he was holding a gun. On this third crossing they went right past Honeymoon Cottage, and didn't stop until they got to Neil's place.

When the Goodmans returned from town they found the Peters sitting on their doorstep, waiting for help. Neil smiled, after he'd heard about their misadventure. "You two...Let's unload these groceries, and then we'll go up there and get you out." While they were in the house, the four sat down for a quick piece of cobbler.

Then Neil and the Peters climbed into Neil's Jeep and bumped all the way up to the spot beyond the end of the road, where the moveable fortress was stuck.

With back-roads expertise Neil whipped up to within fifty feet of their high-centered rig, and then used his truck as an anchor to winch from. It took about fifteen minutes. Neil told them they should get a handyman jack as soon as possible. "Nothin' else'll work up here like a good old American-made high jack."

Kate and Tim promised they would buy one the next time they were in town.

That evening, as the honeymooners curled together inside their cottage Tim suggested an alternate expedition for the following day. "If we can't drive up to the top of the mountain, then tomorrow why don't we head across the creek bottom and check out that far corner of our property on the other side? We can try the mountain again later this summer, after we get a jack."

Agreeing upon the next morning's goal, Tim went to sleep right away. Katie was left to listen to the patter of a summer rain, which started softly and then increased to a steady tapping on the tarpaper roof. It finally pattered her to sleep.

***

Sun up. Birds singing. Today they would drive across the creek, to see what lay on the other side!

Rain showers over, the morning rays on wet grass were making mini-rainbows twinkle and dance everywhere. Kate hummed as she rinsed out the two oatmeal bowls from breakfast, using the remnants of her cup of face washing/tooth brushing water to do the job. By specializing in meals that used only one pan, she had found that she could usually clean up the whole meal using only two cups of water. And the bracing washes outside their cabin door each morning used even less than that. When it came to water, economy was the byword.

When the dishes were drying, Tim took the rifle and Kate grabbed the stove lid, and they both climbed up into the Landcruiser. Tim started 'er up, and steered west directly over the lip of the hill and down the steep bank, to the bottom of the valley. There, a little creek trickled through mossy woods. To the right, Kate saw the barricade of intertwined alder and spruce branches she had piled there in an effort to dissuade any bears from getting too close. Neil had laughed when she told him about it.

"That won't keep a bear from coming in, if that's what he's of a mind to do. He'll just go over it or break through it," Neil had said. He was probably right.

"Here we go," Tim announced, as they began to traverse the uncharted bottomland.

He made the little green machine plunge out into the mud, and kept her nose facing toward the bench of dry land that lay on the far side, twenty feet away. Ten feet into the valiant run their car sank like a boulder and came to rest, tipped up on Tim's side, and burying the top of the fender on Kate's. Tim cantilevered out his window, slid down into the thigh-deep sludge, and stood surveying the damage. Kate followed.

"Hmm," Tim shook his head, appearing to think bad thoughts.

"It's lucky we have both the shotgun *and* the stove lid with us today," Katie said, injecting a bit of humor into the mix. But she could see that at that moment, Tim was nonplussed beyond repair.

The stove lid would be useless, and the winch was buried nose down at the bottom of the mud hole. They'd have to get Neil to help them out. ...Again! "Damn it!" Tim cursed even louder than he had the day before.

When he was feeling a little happier, they helped each other out of the creek bed and climbed up the steep hill, aiming for Goodmans' place.

...It would have been funny, if it hadn't been so darned humiliating.

This time Neil fired up his big bulldozer and beckoned the greenhorns aboard. Sitting way up on top as they headed into battle, Kate's smile was a yard wide. So was Tim's. She couldn't see the driver's face, but he was probably grinning at least.

When they got to the scene of the near disaster, they beat that muck with just one yank of the dozer. That's when Neil said, for the second time in as many days, that they ought to get themselves a real jack.

That afternoon they drove into Footprint and bought the biggest, meanest long-handled handyman jack on the face of the earth. Next time they really *would* be ready!

***

In the middle of July they started construction on their new house! Kate showed Neil where she wanted the front window to be, and he ran his dozer up there and carved a big amphitheater out of the topsoil, right under that moose's bed. Then Tim and Neil got out a transit and "shot the four corners" (a term new to Kate). Tim explained that the house had to be level. On that, he wouldn't budge. He and Neil did some more corner-shooting, and Kate brought cups of water over to them when they got thirsty.

Since he was so particular about the walls being straight and level, it was decided that Tim would be the mason, and Kate would be his hod carrier. Tim would lay the blocks, keeping every round perfectly level, and her job would be to transport everything to the construction site, including cinder blocks, cement, sand and water. To her credit, she worked like a trooper, driving all the way into Footprint and loading and hauling tons of supplies back across the bridge and up the hill, until they had a stack of fourteen hundred cinder blocks waiting to be fashioned into their dream home on top of that mountain.

Meanwhile, the men had been keeping pretty busy with their bulldozer and their transit. Upon delivery of the last load of cement and cinderblocks to the site, Neil leaned against his truck's fender and chuckled. Then he said, "Katie girl, I've watched you going out and comin' back in with that loaded-down trailer, over and over again. And I've been thinking maybe I ought to mention how that bridge might not be able to handle so much weight..." He paused. "The truth is, every time I make it over that bridge I figure I've cheated death just one more time. ...It's about ready to fall in, you know!"

Tim seemed to think that was pretty funny, and he laughed along with Neil.

Kate vowed as how she was glad he hadn't told her before. She was certain her life was all that much fuller for having accomplished the dangerous mission, and she thanked Neil for waiting until its completion.

***

They worked all summer building a firm foundation for their life together.

In early August the Goodmans took Kate to the Alaska State Fair. It was held down in Ninilchik, and it was the biggest shindig of the year. Since there was only room for three people in the cab, and since Tim wasn't much of a livestock fan, he stayed home. Everyone on the entire Kenai Peninsula except Tim, would be there to admire the best of the best.

When they got to the fairgrounds Neil parked the truck out in the pasture with a lot of nearly identical farm rigs, and the three headed directly into the hubbub. The place was hopping with excited cooks displaying their fanciest baked goods and their nicest bottled pickles, and taciturn farmers showing off their fattest pigs, all shined up and squealing. Cowboys were strutting around between the various riding events, with little boys tagging behind them like stable puppies. Everyone was dressed for the festivities in his or her own way.

"Tell me about those ladies in the bright colors. Who are they?" Kate asked Elsie.

"That's the 'Russians'. They come up from Nikiski, a village just down the road," she said. "They left Russia for religious reasons I think, like the Pilgrims."

"Well they get the prize for the most colorful clothing," Kate said, admiring the shiny skirts.

"The men wear Cossack shirts. Keep your eye peeled and you'll see quite a few of 'em around. They usually come to Soldotna in groups."

"Are they sort of like the Amish?"

"I don't know much about the Amish, but these folks stick to their traditional ways and they stay pretty isolated. Most of them only speak Russian."

The community of Nikiski was well represented that day, and one of the scheduled events was a demonstration of dances from their Motherland. The displaced Russians were everywhere; eating cotton candy, dressed in pink and green satins of near fluorescent intensity.

Like the Amish, they didn't appear to appreciate being stared at, but this fair gave ample opportunity for the curious to observe them. They were positively gorgeous, weaving between all the overalls and cowboy hats, wearing their swirling flamboyant colors.

"You may have seen one of their cars," Neil told Kate, "...bright green or orange?"

The memory returned to her. "Yeah, I guess I have, over in Soldotna, in front of the feed store.

"And their houses are painted like that too. They just love those brilliant colors," Elsie said. "One day you two should take the road into Nikiski to see them."

After the rodeo roping and Russian dancing demonstrations had died down, Neil said he was going to go take a look at the bulls. The two women went their own way, into the main tent to study the pickles.

Jostling through the crowds admiring the cakes and pies was tiring, and when the ladies

117

eventually came to the very end of that long tent and spied a pair of recliner chairs sitting there vacant, looking like they were just waiting for a couple of tired women to sit down in them, the ladies gladly sat. Right away a furniture salesman swooped down like a big barn spider. He started talking earnestly to Elsie; because she looked more interested than Kate, who listened as best she could, but couldn't hear what he was saying over the din.

Elsie was listening and smiling and apparently taking everything in. He flipped a switch on the outside of her armchair, and it began to move in little undulating waves up and down. Elsie whooped in genuine surprise. Happy with her reaction, the salesman whipped out a fabric swatch board and showed her all the colors that particular piece of furniture came in. She seemed to like what she saw, and she even reached out and felt one sample's green herringbone pattern. Encouraged, the salesman talked on and on to Elsie, and she continued to tilt her ear toward him and smile. When he showed her a list of interior styles, she pointed to the one called 'early American', and he brightened even more.

Neil finally showed up to rescue the ladies. "Ready to go?" he asked, when he found them at the far end of the longest tent.

Elsie and Katie both nodded and rose from their chairs. They thanked the hovering salesman and escaped with Neil into the graying Alaskan afternoon. Out in the big pasture that served as parking for the event, they stopped and looked around for the Jeep.

"There it is!" Elsie said. It was grazing in a herd of other trucks that looked just like it.

Neil and Elsie opened up the truck doors and aired it out for a minute, and then Kate sat in the middle and they piled in on either side of her. Neil steered slowly around and through the herd of trucks until he could pull out onto the pavement. Then he turned northeast and headed for home.

Once they were out of the fairground, Kate gave Elsie a knowing look. "I thought that chair salesman about had you convinced," she joked, "especially when he promised he would bring up a chair to match your vintage American décor."

"Is that what he said?" Elsie asked, looking surprised.

"You mean you missed that part of the spiel?"

"To tell you the truth Kate, I missed pretty much all of it. It was so loud in there I couldn't hardly hear a word he said."

This was getting better by the minute. "But you were nodding and smiling the whole time," Kate reminded her.

"That's because I was trying to be nice. He was working so hard."

"Now that is funny!" Kate laughed out loud, and then Elsie started laughing too.

By this time Neil was looking concerned. "You didn't sign anything, did you?" he asked Elsie.

"Oh, my heavens, no! I doubt we'll ever see that poor fellow again."

Of course Elsie knew what she was talking about. No furniture salesman in his right mind would drive his truck full of recliners over that bridge to match it with the décor in her house. And besides, she already had plenty of furniture right there in the barn loft.

***

Near the end of August, Neil and Elsie departed for parts unknown. They had decided it was time to move Outside for good. "Outside" was what Alaskan's called the continental United States, the way Hawaiians called it "the Mainland." Claiming that they were getting too old for this kind of life, they were pulling up stakes and heading for the Lower Forty-Eight. This was not happy news for Kate. She loved Elsie. Elsie was the only woman who lived within easy walking distance. If the Goodmans left; their nearest neighbors would be Anne and Brian four miles one way, and Pat and Bill five miles the other way.

But it wasn't a total surprise. Kate had always known that their plan was to subdivide the homestead and sell off enough parcels to fund a cattle ranch start up.

Best to take their departure in stride. Besides, they would be back. As soon as they found a place, Neil said they'd come back to Alaska to pack up everything.

———◇———

*Soon they would be on their own
on that mountain...*

CHAPTER 9
LEAVING ALL THE BULL BEHIND

October. The Goodmans were back. They'd found a piece of ranch land, and Neil planned to be ready to start his new herd come spring. Kate was glad that Elsie would finally be getting her two-room house, but she sure would miss their friendly mentors.

Neil wanted to get out of there before the road fell apart, so the next two weeks were a hurried, emotion-packed time. By the end of October the Goodmans were all packed up, and ready to head south. All of their livestock, the cattle, the sheep, the hogs and the chickens had been redistributed across the region. Only one bay horse still remained on the farm. That was Neil's favorite cow pony. They planned on taking him along. The settlers had passed down a lot of machinery to their heirs-apparent, and the newcomers had also bought their barn full of furniture, several hand tools and a big standup freezer packed with steaks and chops. The two hundred dollar sale price was barely enough to cover the gas for their drive down the Alcan. Neil had taken along everything he thought he'd need to start a new cattle operation. He'd even dismantled the calving barn and packed that! But he'd said there wasn't room for Elsie's canned goods, so they'd given several cases of vegetables to Tim and Kate. There were jams and jellies, and a dozen jars of bull meat that she'd put up. When Kate saw that, she joked that Neil and Elsie really *were* leaving all the bull behind!

After their very last breakfast together, Elsie handed Katie her aluminum tea kettle and the moth-eaten green sweater that had kept her warm over the past twenty years. Kate received them with the respect due a cloak and scepter. Neil gave Kate her very own brand new cowboy hat; and that almost made her tear up. And he told Tim to take both snowmachines, and treat 'em good.

Then the homesteader walked down to the corral, opened the gate and led his horse up to the waiting cattle trailer. He stuffed the hesitant animal

into the back of the load, where his nostrils flared at such a close fit between the calving barn and the branding irons.

Neil took one more look around, and announced it was time to go. All four shook hands, and Katie topped it off with hugs for her dear friends. Then the two old pioneers climbed up into the overstuffed cargo truck, while the two novices stood their ground. One deep breath all around and Neil started the big silver truck moving forward. There was a lot of hand waving. Katie kept calling out good wishes for the trip, and happy trails to them both; and she wanted to cry as she watched the hooked and bulging vehicles slowly make their way down the slushy road.

Kate's final view of that wonderful couple and all that they stood for, was of that bay horse's rear end sticking up over the back end of the trailer. She watched the brown rump sway sideways and jostle up and down as the truck bumped away. ...And then they were gone.

Tim and Kate stared at the empty spot where their beloved friends had just driven out of their lives. After a suitable season of mourning, Tim turned and said, "Well, Baby, are you ready to head home?"

Kate dragged her eyes away from the vanishing point. "I guess so."

"Don't look so lost," Tim said. "We'll be fine. Remember-- if anyone can do it, we can."

"So you say. But it'll be lonely around here without them."

"...Come on, don't worry. If it gets hard, you just hold onto my back pockets. I'll pull you through."

"Okay. ...Are they double-stitched?"

***

As soon as the basement was finished, they intended to start bringing their bounty up the hill. Elsie's home canning: tomatoes, green beans, rhubarb jam and the jars of beef would live in the root cellar they were fashioning. The beautiful old couch and chair, the sleigh bed, and an assortment of books would wait safely in the barn, until they could rest permanently in their new home on top of the mountain.

The young settlers inherited several antique pieces with interesting shapes and mysterious uses, such as the "washing machine" Neil had given Katie. She hadn't yet figured out how to use the cone-on-a-stick tool, and she wasn't sure she ever wanted to. It looked like a torture device.

The two antique snowmachines would stay where they were until the snows began to fall. Then Tim and Kate could ride them home. Out of everything the Goodmans had included in that two hundred dollar outfitting package, Tim thought those two Skidoo® relics might prove to be the most valuable of all.

***

Neil and Elsie had also given them a rusted iron bed that had been leaning outside against the back wall of the saw mill. Kate sanded it and painted it red, and it looked great. She planned to spread their black quilt with pink rosebuds over it. That would make the bed exude a cheery 'welcome home' greeting each time they walked into the basement. And it would look *especially* friendly if they had had a really hard journey home.

Coffee pot? ...Or shotgun??

CHAPTER 10
SHOTGUN BRIDE

"I've changed my mind. I don't think I need to learn how to shoot a gun."

"Out here everyone needs to know how to shoot a gun. If some no-good comes around while I'm gone, you might need to shoot him." Tim was adamant.

"Ha! If some no-good comes around, I'll just run."

"Katie, really bad guys don't stand around watching, while a girl runs off across the prairie. And besides, what if you're up in the woods and a bear comes out of the brush?"

"I'll whistle *Dixie*. That'll scatter the wildlife for miles."

"You can't whistle. Remember?" Tim was already taking the shotgun down from over the door. Apparently the negotiations were over.

He put on his favorite 798er welder's hat, the yellow one with polka-dots, picked up a box of shotgun shells, and ducked under the lintel. "Oh, you might want to bring along a pillow," he called back over his shoulder.

"Okay," Kate acquiesced to the retreating form. He was right, of course. If it ever did come down to it, she *would* have to protect herself, and any little ones they might have running around. So she slung on her jacket, remembered to grab a pillow, and headed up the hill to shotgun school. When she caught up to Tim, he was standing beside one of their three empty fifty-five gallon drums.

"You can use this as a target," he said.

"But we need those barrels for fuel. What good is a barrel with holes in it?"

"We also need a bigger burn barrel," he said, brandishing the shotgun. "Here. Shoot some air holes in it for us."

"Okay. ...But what if I miss? What if I hit the wheel barrow behind it?"

"You won't hit the wheel barrow. It's far enough away. This gun is for close range. You can't miss, as long as you let your target get close enough before you shoot."

Kate frowned. "How close would I want to let a charging bear get before I pull the trigger?"

"About twenty feet; this triple-aught buck will stop anything dead in its tracks at twenty feet."

"But I don't want to kill anything. Isn't there another way to protect ourselves? "

"You mean, like calling in the Troopers? Remember we don't have any way to call for help. And even if we *could* call them, it might take days for them to get here."

This was true.

"You won't be shooting at anything unless it's charging you, in which case you wait till he's right in front of you, then aim and fire."

He paused for emphasis. "...And that goes for man *or* beast."

"I hate this," Kate muttered. But she took the gun from him and followed each one of his directions, concentrating hard, as if her life depended on it. Under his watchful eye she loaded the short-barreled weapon with buckshot and closed the breach with a meek snap.

"Make *sure* it's closed," Tim corrected. "You better open it and close it again."

Kate complied, adding commitment to her second attempt.

"...And now you're loaded for bear," Tim said with a satisfied smile. After that, he demonstrated the proper way to carry a rifle, and Kate hoped the lesson was about over. It hadn't been too bad, actually. That happy thought was cut short when Tim moved right on to part two of the training.

"Now, you see these two hammers here?" He was pointing to a pair of levers that looked like little mouse ears sticking up out of the gun barrel. "You can either cock one, or both barrels. But you'll usually just want to shoot one barrel at a time. That way you still have a second shot, in case you miss your first shot." He took a step back from his bride and reminded her not to cock both of them at once.

"Remember, two together will make one hell of a big kick."

Now things were getting tricky. Wouldn't it be a lot simpler to just burst into a rousing rendition of *Dixie*, and scare the culprit away? Kate had lungs that fired like cannons.

Tim grabbed the pillow off of one of the other empty drums. "Here. Put this in front of your shoulder." He tucked the padding against Kate's shoulder joint. "Be ready for a wallop when you fire."

She didn't feel ready.

Okay. ...Now cock it, and you're ready to shoot."

"I probably won't have a pillow with me," she said, trying to postpone the inevitable.

Tim cut her off. "Go!"

Resigned, Katie very carefully pulled back on the left cocking hammer and raised the weapon. She pressed the gun butt into the pillow that Tim still held against her shoulder, took aim on the empty barrel, pictured it as a charging grizzly and touched the trigger.

BLAM!!

"Ow." Her voice barely squeaked, but her shoulder was singing.

"You did great!" Tim cheered.

He walked over and tapped two little holes in the side of the drum. "See? You hit the bear right here in his shoulder. ...But most of your shot went off to the side. Aim a little more toward the center. Aim right for his heart."

The pioneer's wife hated this whole lesson, but she knew it was something she needed to do. There really was no one else close by who could help, if anything (or anyone) threatening came up their lonely road.

"Okay," Tim said after a moment. "Let's reload. Do you think you're ready to try both barrels at once?"

"Probably not."

The second time, she cocked both mouse ears; and the blast nearly blew Kate over backward. When the smoke cleared, Tim strode up to the can and pointed to a hole the size of a softball, right where the charging bear's throat would have been.

"That's excellent!" he shouted. "...Probably enough practice for today." He took the shotgun from his dazed bride.

"Good." Kate said.

November 4, 1977--Dear Mamasan,

Well I did it! I fired a shotgun! I feel like Alaska Nellie. She's sort of famous around here; a twentieth century version of Annie Oakley. They've still got her old woody Pontiac parked out on the Highway. I'll show you, when you come up. When do you think you can come to visit?

There weren't that many women who lived all alone out in the bush like Alaska Nellie. You would need to be pretty good with a gun, or else you would need a partner who could protect you. If you were part of a team, like Elsie and Neil, then you could *maybe* make a go of it. Kate was thankful that she had Tim, and that he'd been in the war. He would know how to protect her, if necessary. She had entrusted her life to him. In return, she'd do her full share of the labor. They would work together like a pair of strong, well-paired oxen. They would probably be fine.

***

"Timmy?"

They were lying in bed waiting for sleep after yet another killer day. "You want to hear a funny story about Elsie?"

"Um-hum." He would be happy to listen, as long as he didn't have to move.

"Do you know why Elsie never wears a dress?"

"I didn't think she even owned one. In fact, I always suspected they both slept in their boots."

"Ha! Ha! ...No, she owned one, alright. She said she brought one up when they came to Alaska. She told me that Neil used to get after her every now and then, pestering her to put it on. But she always begged off because there was just too much work to be done."

"Hmm. I can see her point."

"Well, one day she finally decided she would surprise him by putting on her dress. While he was out with the livestock, she got all slicked up. Fixed her hair and put on her dress, and dusted off her patent pumps, and all. When he came in, she sashayed around in front of him for a turn or two. ...But all Neil said was, 'Elsie, I need your help for a minute outside.'

Well, Elsie said she was pretty disappointed that he hadn't even noticed. But she knew they were a team (like you and me), so she said, 'Should I change first?'

And this is what really made her fester, because Neil said to her, 'No, don't bother. I just need you to hold that hog while I put a ring in his nose.'"

Kate paused, waiting for a reaction from her mate. But Tim was quiet, so she finished the tale with a flourish, "And that's the last time Elsie ever put on a dress!"

Tim lay there, thoughtful. "I guess this is no place for a woman," he finally said.

"Not one that likes to get gussied-up, anyway," Katie qualified.

Then Tim rolled over and kissed his woman. "So, will you help me cut some firewood tomorrow?"

"Sure. ...Shall I put on a dress?"

EPILOGUE:

By late fall they had the basement finished, and had moved into it. Kate's nephew had come to help, and the three had accomplished the task with no mishaps. Then their nephew went home, and Tim and Kate headed into their first winter alone on the mountaintop.

December 20, 1977– Dear Mamasan,

Greetings from the far North!

Christmas is upon us! We cut down a tree and dragged it home and stood it up in the new basement, so we're all ready for the upcoming festivities. I decorated it with strings of dried wild cranberries and blueberries and little wooden ornaments imported from Italy. We even wound strands of electric lights from top to bottom, just in case a miracle should occur...

Two days before Christmas, a miracle *did* happen when a very odd looking vehicle "stepped" out of the woods and headed up across the field. It was coming toward their house. As soon as Tim saw it, he stopped what he was doing and ran inside.

"What is it?" Kate asked, alarmed. "Do we need the shotgun?"

"No. It's Rural Electric...I think we're getting power!"

Katie wondered if this was one of Tim's jokes, so she went outside to take her own look at a rig that reminded her of a giant mosquito. It had something like jointed legs that seemed to be walking on top of the five-foot deep snow.

Then she saw the lettering. Tim was right! The electric company was paying them a visit! She ran down the steps and burst into the basement.

"I'll put on the coffee pot!" the woman of the house announced.

"You got that right!"

Long ago, Neil had commented on the benefit of their expansive view. "When someone comes up the road, you'll have plenty of time to decide whether to get out the rifle, or the coffee pot," he had said. Kate hadn't believed he was serious then, but she had since come to see that his observation was dead on. It was good to have time to prepare for whatever came out of those woods.

Meanwhile, Tim was moving stuff around on his workbench, looking for the outlet box he'd bought a while back. He found what he needed, and set to work. It would be a race to see if he could finish wiring up his end, before they completed theirs.

Once the cowboy coffee was heating on top of the coal furnace, Kate went back outside and stationed herself to meet the crew when they arrived. As it got closer, she could see that the pachyderm-mosquito-looking thing was really just an oversized tracked vehicle. It said 'Rural Electric' on it, clear as day.

As the machine came to a stop she said, "You gentlemen sure are a welcome sight. Are you here to hook up our electricity?"

Four men smiled down at her. "Yes Ma'am," said the spokesman of the group.

"Oh, that's wonderful!! My husband's inside installing a light box, as we speak."

"Well that's good, 'cause it won't take us long to get you some power. We should be done pretty quick."

Kate was overcome with gratitude. "Oh, thank you so much! You can't imagine how glad we are to be getting power, at last. We've been on the waiting list for a year and a half." Even as she said this, she knew that these men were well aware of how much their service was appreciated. "Would you like to come in for coffee when you get finished out here?"

"We sure would. Thanks," the crew boss said.

After a while, the men came inside to warm up; and they polished off a whole pot of coffee while visiting with Tim and Kate.

"You folks are now the end of the line," one of the men said.

"Yay!" Kate was thrilled, and she told them this was the best day in her life. But the four men sat there calmly, like this was just another day at work. She guessed that for them, maybe it was!

After half an hour the crew buttoned and zipped up their Carhartt coveralls, and headed back out to finish hooking up the Peters' line. That part of the procedure went really fast; and before Kate knew it, she heard the huge machine starting up. She ran outside, and got there just in time to hear the crew boss call out something from his seat high atop the weird sleigh. "Merry Christmas, from Rural Electric!" he shouted.

Then the huge thing backed up, rocked to a stop for a quick gear change, and began its awkward walk down the mountain.

"They're gone," Kate said as she ducked back inside.

"Let's try this out, and see if we've got any power," Tim said. He plugged a trouble lamp into the box he'd just finished wiring.

...The bulb blazed with light! Katie danced and hooted, and Tim basked in the glory.

Katie couldn't wait. "Where's another extension cord? We need to try plugging in the Christmas tree!"

Since they'd never, until that moment had any power to extend, finding a second cord took some time. Tim finally found a paint-stained one in a miscellaneous box Neil had handed down. He plugged in one end for the tree lights, and paused to wait for Kate to get ready to witness the wondrous sight.

"Would you care to do the honors?" he offered.

"No, you go ahead. I'll just watch."

"Tell me when you're ready."

"Let the games begin!" Kate cried.

Tim plugged in the extension cord... and the festooned tree shot to life. It was a sight to behold, a glowing symbol of hope and peace. Its beauty would shine out through their window, to temper the pitch black of night.

December 26, 1977 – Dear Mamasan,

Late Merry Christmas and early Happy New Year to you! Thank you for the huge bowl, and the wonderful blankets. We opened them yesterday, and they're perfect. I promised Tim I would try baking bread as soon as we get an oven. This bowl will be great for mixing and kneading. And of course we can always use the blankets. Your packing job was ingenious. News flash: We've got electricity!! It was Rural Electric's Christmas gift to us!

Dear Mamasan,

Guess what!
I'm writing this by
light bulb!!

By the time my parents got that electricity, they had already carted and carried fourteen hundred cinder blocks, a hundred bags of cement; triple that of sand and countless milk cans full of water over the old bridge and up to the house site. They'd hand mixed enough concrete to build ten bunkers, cut beams to support the roof and finally moved into that brand new basement.

I'll tell you all the construction details in the next book. But for now, let's just say, they were elated to have power. ...And just before Christmas, too. How wondrous!

A.C.

Two days after Christmas, the Cheechakos headed into Footprint. They went to the Coffee Café and had breakfast. Then they took showers, did laundry, bought a fancy new citizen's band radio with a ten foot antenna, got groceries and filled the water cans. They went to the post office on the way through Sleeping Moose, mailed off the letter to Kate's mother, picked up two Christmas cards and a copy of the Birch Society's *Spotlight News* that waited for them courtesy of Neil, and drove across the highway to the place where folks were parking those days.

They parked near the other road vehicles and transferred everything into the sled that was hooked behind their hand-me-down snowmachine. They climbed aboard and headed up a perfectly smooth, snow-covered driveway. Encountering no problems or complications, the two made it home at dusk.

***

By the next evening "Victory Garden" had become the newest blip on the Sleeping Moose airwaves, and Tim and Kate had already started getting an insider's earful on what was happening on every farm outside of town. Whenever Tim had the volume turned up, all sorts of cryptic messages squawked out into the kitchen.

"'Belle of the Ball,' calling 'Windy Ranch.' Come in. Over."

"This is 'Windy Ranch.' What's up, Dorothy? Over."

"Have you seen Walter down your way? He needs to pick up those two goats before he heads home for supper. Over."

"He's over to Crestman's Ridge. I'll tell Jim to tell 'im, when he gets there. ...Say, are you plannin' on goin' to the equipment auction at 28 mile? Over."

"Not sure yet. It depends on the weather. Over."

...And so on, through the long winter night.

THE END

Dear Reader-
Thank you for choosing to read Volume 1 of this series of nearly true stories. I hope you enjoyed it.

The entire saga: *Tales from Sleeping Moose,* an odyssey about late Twentieth Century pioneering will be available by the end of 2015. Find all four volumes at Amazon.com, Kindle, and at select book sellers.

Happy Reading!
Atwood Cutting

BASIC ALASKAN TERMINOLOGY

"Bush" Alaskan wilderness

"Go-molly" Hiding the dishes until they can be gotten to later

"Cheechako" A newcomer to Alaska

"Sourdough" Someone who's been in Alaska long enough to have grown sour on the place, but doesn't have enough dough to get out

"The Lower Forty-Eight" The contiguous states

"Outside" Same as above

"Outside" Where most bush folks usually go to the bathroom

"Going outside" Leaving the mountain for winter jobs

"Hawaii" Alaskans' favorite place to go in winter

"End of the roaders" Folks who eschew normal society for a variety of reasons, and choose to live as far away from people as they can get

ABOUT THE AUTHOR

Atwood Cutting was born of parents both idealistic and impetuous. She spent her first decade on a remote mountain top in Alaska, and she loved it! Cutting graduated *Phi Beta Kappa*, majoring in the visual and performing arts, and later earned a Master of Liberal Arts degree in Museum Education. She now lives in Colorado.

Writing Volume 1 of this saga, *Alaska Mid-Century Pioneers*, involved researching all of her mother's letters written to her own "Mamasan" in Hawaii while they pioneered in Sleeping Moose, as well as combing through all of the family photograph albums from that time. Of course, the author's biggest source of material was the stories her mother used to tell her about the weather, the road and the neighbors up on Round Top Mountain.

All four volumes of the *Tales from Sleeping Moose* series are available through Amazon.com. www.atwoodcutting.com for more information.

www.ingramcontent.com/pod-product-compliance
Lightning Source LLC
Chambersburg PA
CBHW070334130626
46556CB00007B/2863